Double Clear

Also by Kate Lattey

PONY JUMPERS

#1 First Fence

#2 Double Clear

#3 Triple Bar

#4 Four Faults

#5 Five Stride Line

#6 Six to Ride

#7 Seventh Place

#8 Eight Away

#9 Nine Lives

Special Edition #1 Jonty

DARE TO DREAM

#1 Dare to Dream

#2 Dream On

CLEARWATER BAY

#1 Flying Changes

#2 Against the Clock

For more information, visit nzponywriter.com

Email nzponywriter@gmail.com and sign up to my mailing list for exclusive previews, new releases, giveaways and more!

Pony Jumpers

#2

DOUBLE CLEAR

Kate Lattey

1st Edition (print).

Cover photo: Paula Riepen.

This is a work of fiction. Names, characters, places and incidents are either the product of the author's imagination or are used fictitiously.

ISBN-13: 978-1539838999

ISBN-10: 1539838994

\- ♥ \-

If riding were only blue ribbons and bright lights
I would have quit a long time ago.

George Morris

\- ♥ \-

1
DOUBLE TROUBLE

The rain was coming down in sheets, turning the ponies into misty outlines as they grazed in their paddocks, their hindquarters to the wind. I pushed the dripping hair out of my eyes and dragged a heavy cover down from its rack in the tack room, then walked back out to where Molly was standing in her stable, finishing her feed.

She looked up at me as I opened her door, her delicately-curved ears swivelling in my direction. Lifted her bran-coated muzzle from the feed bucket, and watched me approach with the warm rug over my arm.

"All done?" I asked her, peering into her bucket. "Come on, eat up."

A layer of bran still covered the bottom of the bucket, and clumps of pony nuts were pushed into the corners. Molly swished her tail at me and lowered her nose back into the feed, lipping delicately at it. She'd always been a picky eater, but she got worse the more work she was in. By the end of the competition season, I had to leave her with a feed for a couple of hours before she'd finish it up. But it was only October, and the fussiness didn't usually start this early.

"Get with the program Mollypop," I grumbled at her as I threw the heavy cover over her back.

She was still growing out her clip and needed a bit of help to stay warm. And I couldn't afford to let her get cold, especially if she wasn't going to eat properly.

Molly lifted her head out of the bucket again and snorted, spraying bits of bran mash onto my face.

"That's great, thanks," I told her as I buckled the front straps and tugged her neck rug into place. "Who needs an oatmeal scrub when I have a pony as disgusting as you?"

The porch light came on – Mum's signal to me that it was time to come inside. I dropped a kiss onto Molly's nose, and she dribbled more bran onto my neck.

"You're my best girl," I told her. "Finish up your dinner and I'll let you out once I've had mine."

Yanking my hoodie up over my head, I turned and ran across the yard, dodging puddles on the way to the house. Critter yapped at me as I kicked the front door open and went inside.

"There you are," Mum said, glancing up from the couch. "I thought you'd drowned out there or something."

"Funny." I peeled my wet hoodie off and sat down at the table to unzip my chaps. "Moll's not eating again."

Mum groaned. "That pony, honestly. I knew she was called Double Trouble for a reason."

"Hey, be nice. We're lucky to have her."

That was the understatement of the century, as far as I was concerned, and Mum didn't argue. I pulled my paddock boots off and threw them into the corner by the door, followed by my soggy chaps. My socks squelched slightly as I crossed the kitchen floor and filled a glass of water from the tap.

"Dinner's in the microwave," Mum told me. "Butter chicken."

"I'm not really hungry."

I sat down at the kitchen table and looked at my schoolbag, overflowing with assignments and essays and exemplars. Usually by this time of the year I had all of that under control, needing only a handful of credits to pass my subjects, but I'd been so busy over winter riding the schoolers and breakers that Mum had kept bringing in that I'd fallen behind. Now I was in danger of actually failing a couple of subjects. Not that Mum knew that. Not yet, anyway.

"You're as bad as that pony," Mum grumbled. "Go on, I'll heat your food while you shower."

I peeled my wet socks off and left them under the table. "I'll shower before bed. I need to get started on this."

I opened my bag and looked critically at the pile of paperwork.

"Dinner first, Katy."

Mum's voice was insistent, and I knew she wouldn't shut up until I did as I was told, so I got reluctantly to my feet and went to the microwave. *8:25.* When did it get so late? I pressed the buttons to reheat my meal, then looked across the yard towards the stables. The light was still on in Molly's box, but she was standing at the door, looking plaintively out into the night.

"Moll's not going to eat. I'll go turn her out," I said, but Mum stood up.

"I'll do it. You eat *your* dinner. Do you have homework to do?"

If you only knew. "Yeah, a bit."

"Get on with it then."

Mum pulled on her gumboots and shouldered herself into her large, smelly oilskin before heading back out into the rain. The microwave beeped as she left, but I already had my schoolwork laid out in front of me, so I ignored it.

Moments later, the phone rang. I tried to ignore that too, hoping it would go straight to voicemail, but when it rang again only seconds after it stopped, I gave in and picked it up.

"Hello?"

"Have you heard the news?" It was my best friend AJ, and she sounded upset.

"What news?"

"Oh my God. About Samantha Marshall. You know her, right? Because of Molly?"

"Right..."

Sam's family had bred and still owned Molly. She'd been ridden by Sam's younger sister Steph from break-in through to the start of her competition career, but although she came from a long and distinguished line of Grand Prix ponies, she'd never jumped very well for Steph, so had been consigned to their broodmare paddock. When repeated attempts to get her in foal had failed, Mum had talked Steph's mother Kat, an old friend of hers, into letting us lease her. We'd expected that Molly would give me some good mileage at the lower heights, but I'd never had a problem convincing her to jump well, and we'd taken on the Grand Prix circuit after only a few months together. She would never be a completely easy or consistent pony, but we'd won some big classes, and she'd taught me more than any other pony I'd ever had.

"What's happened to Sam?"

"She fell off on the cross-country at Burghley."

"What?" Unlike her sister, who was a show jumper through and through, Sam was a keen three-day event rider. One of the most promising young riders New Zealand had ever seen, and only a few months ago, her top ten finish at Badminton had cemented her spot in the upcoming Olympic squad. "Is she okay?"

"I don't know," AJ admitted. "They're not saying, but it doesn't look good. She's not dead," she quickly clarified as my blood turned to ice. "But it was a rotational fall. The horse flipped right over on top of her, and they think she's broken her neck."

My heart was pounding. "How do you know this?"

"It's all over Facebook, and the news, and everywhere. How do you *not*?"

Mum came back inside just then, and I told AJ I had to go, then swiftly broke the news to my mother.

"Sam Marshall fell off at Burghley, and they think she's broken her neck."

The words sounded unreal coming out of my mouth, and Mum turned white as I spoke. She grabbed the phone from me and dialled frantically. I knew she would be trying to get hold of Sam's mum, but I doubted her chances.

"They've probably taken the phone off the hook," I told her, then caught a glimpse of a horse on the TV. We both hurried towards the screen, and I quickly turned the sound back on.

"…riding an up-and-coming horse called Monkey Trouble for his British owners, and had jumped strongly around the course before the fall at fence eighteen. Earlier in the day,

Marshall rode a clear round on her own horse Kingdom Come, one of only three riders to come home within the time allowed."

I watched in sick trepidation as the footage showed Sam riding confidently down to a huge solid oxer on a strong bay horse. They looked perfect, the horse cantering strongly, Sam expertly balanced in the saddle. And then the horse tripped, losing his footing at the base of the jump. The footage went into slow motion, and I gasped as Monkey Trouble lifted off and almost made it, until his forelegs hit the massive wooden log, catapulting his huge body through the air. His hind legs came up over his head and he flipped right over, cannoning into the turf. Sam was still in the saddle as several hundred kilos of horseflesh landed on her slender frame, slamming her into the ground beneath him.

"Marshall is in critical condition in hospital, with suspected neck and spinal fractures. Whether she will make a full recovery is unknown, but experts reviewing the footage consider it to be unlikely. The horse suffered a broken shoulder, and was euthanized at the scene."

"Have you heard anything from the Marshalls?"

I looked at AJ as she sat down next to me at school the next day, and shook my head. "Nothing. Mum's been trying to get through, but no luck so far."

"What a terrible thing to have happened."

"Tragic," I agreed. "I still can't believe it."

"What if she can't ever walk again?" AJ said sadly.

"What if she can't ever *ride*?"

AJ gave me a strange look, which I tried to shrug off. I knew that it sounded weird to consider walking less important than riding, but I couldn't think of Sam not being on horseback. There are people who look good on a horse, and then there are people who look as though they were born on a horse. People who, when you see them walking around on their own feet, look like just another ordinary person. But when you see them in the saddle, they become confident and self-possessed – like a different person altogether.

I've felt that way myself sometimes. At school, wearing my stupid uniform and walking through the halls filled with other people, all so much smarter and prettier and more confident than me, I would imagine myself on horseback. I'd picture Molly's pricked ears in front of me, or Lucas's arched neck with its short flaxen mane. I'd imagine their confident, swinging length of stride, and hold myself straighter and walk taller, filled with a sense of purpose and competence. Feeling like a complete person, strong and capable and ready to take on the world, if only there was a horse under me.

I was sure that Sam felt that way too. I'd only met her a handful of times, but she was always nice, friendly and quick to offer encouragement and praise. Everyone loved her – horses included. Everyone said she could've jumped a donkey around Badminton, and I wondered how it had all gone so terribly wrong.

Lucas's chestnut ears were pricked ahead of me as I cantered across the diagonal of the arena. Three strides, two strides, one stride out of the corner and I asked for a flying change. Lucas gave it to me as always, but he was late behind, and took one disunited step before correcting himself. I gritted my teeth as I balanced him around the turn, waiting for Mum to comment.

It didn't take long.

"He was late behind," she called from her vantage point on the long side, sitting on an oil drum turned sideways with Critter panting at her feet.

"I *can* tell for myself. I'm not a beginner."

I turned Lucas away from Mum, still cantering, and circled him in the corner. Focused hard on having him pushing through from behind, working that inside hind leg, bending through his body yet staying light and supple in the contact. I could feel him focusing beneath me, trying so hard to do what I was asking of him. I blocked out Mum's continuing barrage of criticism and aimed Lucas back across the diagonal. This time, I let his canter out a little as we went, wrapping my legs around his sides and powering him up, letting his stride get quicker and stronger as we crossed the middle of the arena. Sat down and looked right and prepared for the turn, then slid my outside leg back and shifted my weight slightly to the right. Lucas executed a flawless flying change onto the right lead.

"Good boy," I told him, letting my inside hand shift forward to touch his withers as gentle praise, and Lucas arched his neck slightly in response.

Molly had taught me that technique. She didn't appreciate overenthusiastic patting, and the first time I'd tried to praise her with the conventional firm slaps on her neck for a job well done, she'd thrown her head up and given me a nosebleed. That'd only had to happen a couple of times before I'd discovered that less was more with her, and softened my approach. The habit had gradually translated over to my other ponies, who all seemed to appreciate it too. As it turned out, horses preferred a gentle rub to an open-handed whack. Not rocket science, if you thought about it, but it had taken Molly complaining to make me work it out. There were a lot of things I'd taken for granted before she came into my life, but everything she'd taught me had made me a much better rider, even if I'd had to learn them through a lot of trial and error.

Lucas made another perfect flying change back onto the left lead, and I eased him back to a walk, letting the reins out onto his neck and scratching his withers with my fingertips.

"Good job." Mum looked out across the arena towards our yard, where a big black Range Rover had just driven in. "Who's this?"

I shrugged, kicking my feet free of the stirrups and circling Lucas. "Wasn't someone coming to look at Robin?"

"They cancelled."

"I wish they hadn't." I let one hand rest on my thigh as I rode Lucas in a smaller circle, using my seat and leg to steer him. I held the reins one-handed and high, pretending I was a Western rider on a stock horse. Lucas lowered his head obligingly, playing his part. "I can't wait to get rid of that pony."

"Don't you dare talk like that about him when they do show up," Mum cautioned me, and I rolled my eyes.

"I'm not stupid. We have sold ponies before, you know."

Mum and I had spent the past few years patching together additional income by buying cheap ponies, producing them well and selling them on at a profit. We always had several on the go, and when I was younger no pony was safe from being sold out from under me. Even my good ponies, the ones that had been bought with the intention to keep them and let me have a shot at the big time, had left when the money got too good. Reebok and Johnny and Tucker and Spice. Bart, Coffee, Kiwi and little Prancer. Every time, Mum had promised me that the money would go on an even better pony, but somehow it never had. We'd always needed something else more, and she could never let a cheap prospect pass her by.

Molly had been the first pony to come on long-term lease, unable to be sold on, and Lucas had followed a year later. They were the only two on the property that were safe. Puppet was also a lease, but I already knew he wasn't going to get to stick around, because his owners had some wild aspiration that their twelve-year-old daughter Lacey was going to be capable of riding him some day. Considering Lacey was one of those kids who cried if her pony cantered, and wouldn't jump more than a crossbar, the very thought of her sitting on a pony as sensitive and talented as Puppet broke my heart, but it wasn't something I could do anything about.

"Can you see who it is?" Mum asked as we heard a car door slam, and I turned in the saddle and squinted from my higher vantage point. A man in a black windbreaker and grey jeans was standing in the yard, talking to AJ as she brushed out Squib's white tail.

"Some guy," I told Mum. "Probably trying to sell us something we don't need."

I watched AJ turn and point towards the arena, right at me. The man's eyes followed her arm, and he saw me. After nodding a brief thanks to my friend, he turned and started walking towards us, and something in the pit of my stomach turned to ice. I knew that man. I looked at Mum, and she saw the panic on my face.

"What?"

I couldn't say it out loud. She would see soon enough, when he stepped around the other side of the flax bushes and appeared in the gateway of our arena. I kept my head turned away from him, watching her face instead and waiting to gauge her reaction. I was probably wrong. I had to be. *Because it couldn't be…*

"Lionel," Mum breathed, and my heart thudded again.

He strode towards us as though nothing was wrong, as though he hadn't walked out on us several years ago and left us to fend for ourselves, because he had met a younger, blonder, fitter and far less horse-obsessed woman than my mother, and decided that actually, he didn't want to be a father or a husband after all.

I kept glancing at Mum, watching the tight lines pinching around the edges of her mouth as her eyes narrowed, and I moved Lucas right up next to her and drew him to a halt. Mum reached out and put a hand on my pony's neck, and Lucas raised his head and watched Dad approach, picking up on our tension.

I dropped my fingers to his withers and gave him a reassuring scratch. I couldn't make my problems into his.

Dad spoke first. "Hello."

"What do you want?" I asked, butting in before Mum could speak.

Her fingers clutched at Lucas's short mane, and he turned

and touched her with his muzzle reassuringly. Critter hovered around Mum's ankles, growling tentatively at my father.

"I came to see you."

"Did you just? Well excuse us for not rolling out the red carpet."

"Katy."

Mum's voice was a warning, and I glared down at her. *Don't you dare treat him with respect,* I wanted to yell at her. If there was one fault that my mother had, it was being too nice to people. After what my father had done, walking out without a backwards glance and barely contacting us in the years since, he didn't deserve her respect, and he sure as hell didn't deserve her forgiveness.

"What?" I asked her, but she ignored me.

"I came to let you know that I'm moving back," Dad said. "Well, I've moved back actually. Left Aussie a couple of weeks ago. Haven't bought a place yet, but I'm looking. I'd like to be close by, if possible."

He smiled at me, as though I was going to fling myself off my pony and into his arms. As if all those years and miles that had come between us could be wiped out in an instant, but I just stared at him, unable to believe my ears.

"What makes you think we want you anywhere near us?"

He looked surprised by my reaction, and I wanted to punch him and kick him and scream at him for being so stupid. "I'm your father, Kate."

"No you're not," I told him emphatically, nudging Lucas forward and steering him past the tall, lanky man in the middle of my arena. "Now go away and leave us alone."

2
IT GETS WORSE

"You're being weirdly quiet."

I rolled onto my stomach and looked at AJ as our horse truck rattled down the highway towards the Foxton Racecourse. It was early on Saturday morning, so early that it was still dark outside, and we were on our way to a weekend of show jumping. And after the week I'd had, I was more than ready for a dose of healthy competition, to take my mind off everything else.

"Just sleepy, I guess," AJ said with a shrug.

"Well, if you want sleep I suggest you get it now, because once we arrive it's going to be all hands on deck," I told her, glancing past her at the dividing wall that separated our accommodation from the row of ponies standing in the back, hidden from our sight.

AJ's exuberant grey pony Squib was just the other side of that wall, standing next to Molly and Lucas. My six-year-old dark bay gelding Forbes was there, and Robin, the boring bay gelding that we were hoping to sell as a Show Hunter pony, because he was far too dull and uninspiring to ever have much chop as a show jumper. Even four-year-old Puppet had come along, filling up the last space on the truck and about to have his first overnight experience at a show. I planned to ride him around between classes and give him a taste of the atmosphere, and maybe canter him around a couple of low classes if I had time. It was always good for the young ponies to have an outing without too much pressure – it gave them a positive experience and ensured that they looked forward to their next event.

I closed my eyes and tried to doze, taking my own advice. This was going to be a frantic, non-stop weekend, but that was how I wanted it. I didn't need a spare moment to be thinking about anything other than course plans and clear rounds and whether my prize money would pay back my entries this week.

"I have to tell you something."

I opened one eye and looked at AJ. "Go on then."

"You're not going to like it."

"Try me."

"It's about your dad."

She had my attention now, and I sat up and looked at her. "What about him?"

"I…" She looked nervous. "I think he might be coming to the show this weekend."

"What?" I blinked at her, my head reeling. "How does he know–"

"It just kind of slipped out when he turned up the other day," AJ admitted. "I'm sorry! But I didn't even know he was your dad, and–"

I cut her off. "How exactly does something like that just slip out?" I asked her angrily. "You only talked to him for about thirty seconds!"

AJ hastened to explain, tripping over her own words. "Well

I was brushing out Squib's tail, and he asked me if I was keeping it clean for a special occasion, and I said we're going show jumping at Foxton this weekend, and he asked if Squib was much of a jumper, and I said yes but not as good as your ponies, and he asked if you were riding at Foxton too and I said yes. I had no idea who he was, Katy. I wouldn't have said anything if I'd known how you felt about him."

"So you thought he was a total stranger, but you still filled him in on my life?" I couldn't believe it. "Aren't you the daughter of a detective? Shouldn't you be more wary of random people questioning you?"

"Katy." Mum's voice came from the front seat of the truck, reminding me that she could overhear our conversation. She adjusted her hands on the wheel and glanced in the rear view mirror at me. "She didn't know."

"But⬚"

"It's done now," Mum said. "And if he does turn up, I can ask him to leave."

"You can *tell* him, is what you can do," I replied. "I don't want him hanging around. God!" I lay back down on the sofa, fuming. "He abandons us and moves to Australia, conveniently forgetting that we even exist, and then comes swanning back when his girlfriend dumps him and just expects us to take him back with open arms? Who the hell does he think he is?"

I knew from the start that it was not going to be my best show, and it just kept getting worse as the day went on. I couldn't even use Dad's presence as an excuse, because there was no sign of him at all on Saturday. But the omnipresent shadow of his potential arrival was very off-putting, and I rode badly. I picked up a couple of low ribbons in the Show Hunters on Robin, but completely stuffed up the Championship round. The other ponies all had rails, and the only highlight ended up being AJ's super double clear in the metre-ten on Squib. She rode a cracker and finished third, which should have put me in a great mood. After years of training ponies, the shine had long since come off my own successes in the lower rings, but helping AJ and watching her improve gave me a buzz like no other. Yet somehow even that felt flat.

But there was still the Pony Grand Prix to come on Sunday morning, and I could *not* let anything stuff that up. It was the pinnacle of every show for me, the most prestigious class at the highest level of pony show jumping. It always had the biggest prize money and the fiercest competition, not to mention the highest jumps. Nothing ever meant more at a show than doing well in the Grand Prix, and although I'd put Molly wrong at the double in the 1.20m on Saturday morning, and given Lucas an appalling ride to the oxer in the 1.25m jump off on Saturday afternoon, I had my game face on by the time the Grand Prix rolled around.

AJ was saddling Molly for me as I screwed in Lucas's studs. I crouched next to him, resting his hoof on my knee and painstakingly re-tapped the thread.

"These are getting pretty worn," I told Mum as she slung Lucas's tack over the railing in the covered yards. "Definitely time for a new set on his next rotation. When's Don coming down next to do refits?"

"Couple of weeks yet," Mum told me. "Are you sure you

can't get a bit more mileage out of those?"

I shook my head as I fitted the spanner around the sides of the stud and pulled it around towards me. "Nope, these shoes are wearing out at the toes anyway, and these threads are completely shot." I pulled harder on the spanner, and Lucas shifted his weight, unimpressed. "Sorry buddy. Once more around, and they'll be snug as a bug."

I was just finishing up when I heard my mother's voice in a low hiss. "You can't *be* here."

My heart sank as I dropped Lucas's hoof back to the ground and turned to see my father standing in front of my pony. Lucas reached over the railings and nuzzled him hopefully, his pink muzzle rummaging around Dad's pockets as I straightened up.

"Get out of it," I grumbled at my pony, putting a hand on his chest and shoving him backwards as Dad tried to reach up and pat his face. "Leave him alone," I told my father. "Leave all of us alone. What are you doing here?"

"I came to watch you ride. Not a criminal offence, is it?"

"It is to me. I don't want you here."

Mum was muttering at him, trying to persuade him to walk away and leave us be. AJ was watching me from the next yard, her expression guilty as her eyes flickered between me and my parents. I turned away from all of them and grabbed Lucas's saddle off the railing, slinging it onto his back in one swift motion. Focusing only on that, on making sure that the saddle blanket was completely flat and the gel pad was sitting in just the right place, I slid the saddle back into position.

My parents' voices grew louder and I ducked around to the other side of my pony to avoid them. Out of the corner of my eye, I saw a dark bay pony come to a halt next to Lucas's yard, and I turned to see Susannah Andrews sitting on her experienced show jumper Buckingham, staring at my bickering parents. She was kitted out in all the top brands, money just oozing from her and her pony alike. Her parents were right behind, her father leading her second mount, the gorgeous chestnut Skybeau, also rigged up to the nines. Both of her ponies were top notch, pushbutton rides. The kind of ponies that a five-year-old could ride, completely fool-proof and absolute winning machines. They were the only type of pony she'd ever owned, because her parents only cared about winning. Everyone knew just how far they'd gone in the past to ensure that their darling daughter won, and as a result, most of the other pony riders on the Grand Prix circuit steered pretty well clear of them. Nobody wanted to incite their wrath, and face the potential consequences. Their last attack on a rival's pony had been unsuccessful, at least in terms of taking them out of contention, but we all knew that the pony still bore the scars.

Susannah glanced at me, then back to my parents, whose argument was blocking her progress down the sand aisle that ran between the covered yards. I decided not to care. *Let her wait.* I went back to the other side of Lucas and snugged up his girth, then reached for his bridle, which was hanging over the yard railing.

Susannah's pony Buck reached out a friendly nose to Lucas, and they sniffed each other briefly before I elbowed Lucas in the chest, pushing him back so I could get his bridle on.

"Are they going to be long?" Susannah asked me, nodding

towards my parents.

I narrowed my eyes at her tone. "Sorry, are we in your way? Should we part like the Red Sea to let you through? Mum!" I turned and looked at my mother, whose head swivelled towards me. "You're in her Highness's way. Her entourage are trying to get past."

Susannah's eyebrows drew closer together as she frowned at me, but I couldn't care less what she thought of me anyway. I watched in relief as Dad finally threw up his hands in a gesture of defeat and walked away down the aisle, and Mum came back over to me.

Susannah looked down her nose at us as she nudged her pony into a walk, then said something to AJ as she rode past. I shot a glance over my shoulder at my friend, trying to give her a warning look, but she was smiling at Susannah. *Hopeless.*

I'd tried to explain to AJ why she should despise Susannah, and avoid her like the plague, but somehow the notion of her being a vile person who would purposely wound other people's ponies wasn't getting through AJ's thick skull. Like my mother, she had this weird propensity to dole out forgiveness to people who didn't deserve it. At least Mum was standing up to Dad though. Maybe she was going to turn out to have a spine after all.

I rubbed Molly's crest proudly as she cantered back through the finish flags after her clear round, and she arched her neck, pleased with herself. Drawing her back to a steady trot, I turned towards the gate where Tessa Maxwell was coming in on her sister's grey pony Misty Magic. Misty was entering the ring in his usual fashion, bounding sideways in unseating leaps, and Tessa's face was white and scared. Hayley leaned over the wooden railing, her thick mane of curly blond hair billowing down her back.

"Sit up and get your *leg* on!" she yelled at Tess, who appeared to simply be clinging on for dear life.

I walked Molly back through the gate and pulled her up next to Mum, who was standing alongside Hayley. She handed me a water bottle, and I took it gratefully, swigging back a mouthful as I watched Tess aim Misty at the first jump.

"Get him *straight*!" Hayley cried as the pony approached the oxer on an angle, baulked, then put in a huge effort, springing into the air and somehow clearing the jump.

Tess was clinging onto his mane and looking utterly terrified as he landed. She lost a stirrup, and tried and failed to get it back. Hayley was shouting at her to kick on, but Tess pulled Misty out from the second jump and circled him, trying to get her stirrup back rather than jump a fence without it.

Hayley swore loudly and slapped her palms down on the railing in disgust, making Molly jump. She turned to look at her, and then glanced up at me.

"Sorry. But Tess is doing my head in, honestly! What is *wrong* with her?"

She's terrified of riding a very difficult pony, I wanted to point out, but I said nothing. There was no point in disagreeing with Hayley, because she'd just bulldoze her opinion over top of you if you tried.

"You had a good round. Molly's jumping well," she added idly as she kept an eye on her sister, who was riding Misty back to the second fence, both feet jammed securely into her stirrups.

Misty baulked, Hayley started yelling again and Molly's sensitive ears swivelled back and forth, her skin shivering with tension. I picked up my pony's reins, wanting to get her out of the firing line before Hayley's histrionics upset her too much. She needed to be walked off anyway, to cool down her muscles, so I turned her around, only to come face-to-face with my father.

"I thought you were leaving."

I nudged Molly forward, but he stepped up and blocked her in. If she'd been any other pony, I'd have just ridden over the top of him, but I knew that Molly would freak out if I tried.

"You rode beautifully out there," he told me, pretending as though he was a supportive and caring parent who actually gave a rat's ass about me, when I knew full well that he didn't.

"What would you know about it?" I snapped back.

There was a groan and some more swearing from behind me, and I glanced over my shoulder to see Tess jogging Misty back towards the gate as the bell rang for elimination. The pony's neck was lathered in sweat and he pranced sideways, rolling his eyes at Hayley as if to say *Is this really what I have to put up with now?* Hayley echoed the sentiment, immediately laying into her sister, who charged directly past her and rode off, much to Hayley's disgust.

"That girl, honestly. I could kill her! If I didn't love Misty so much, I'd sell him, but I promised him I never would. If Tess would just harden up and ride like a person and not like a sock puppet, she might get somewhere. He's not *that* hard to ride!"

I did my best to tune out her raving as I looked around for AJ, finally spotting her leading Lucas around on the other side of the warm-up area.

"I have to go," I told my father.

He looked like he was going to argue, but then Hayley stepped up on the other side of Molly and put a hand on her neck, making my pony tremble again. *So sensitive.* I rubbed the base of her mane reassuringly as Hayley spoke.

"I was meaning to ask you, how's Sam? I mean, have you heard anything?"

I shook my head. "Not much. Mum talked to Steph a couple of days ago. Kat's gone over to the UK to be with Sam, and her dad's heading over tomorrow. Steph's staying home to look after the horses, at least in the interim. But she just said what they've been saying on the news, that Sam's in critical condition and her injuries are serious."

Mum said Steph had sounded upset, and she hadn't liked to pry any further. She'd offered her condolences, and the other usual niceties – *If there's anything we can do...Don't hesitate to ask...You've done so much for us, we'd love to repay the favour...* But Steph had assured her that she was fine. Mum didn't really believe her, but there was nothing left that she could do except hope that Steph would call her if she needed her help. It was a wish that Mum expressed on a regular basis. Out loud, to me, as though it was a sentiment that I didn't share. I did, of course, but I couldn't see what we possibly had to offer Steph that she couldn't get from someone else much closer to her. Still, I nodded along agreeably whenever Mum brought it up.

"Let us know if you find out anything more," Hayley said,

and I told her that I would, which was a blatant lie because Hayley was the biggest gossip out; not to mention the fact that she barely knew Sam, who had based herself in the UK three years ago and rarely returned to New Zealand.

But I made the false promise and managed to manoeuvre Molly past her and around my father, and then I was finally able to ride over to where my other pony was waiting.

"Swap ya," I told AJ, jumping down from Molly's back and taking over Lucas's reins. We made the exchange quickly, and soon I was on board Lucas and trotting away, trying to clear my mind of everything except the pony under me and the course ahead.

"Woah," I murmured under my breath as Lucas powered down the line towards the planks.

I checked him back once, twice, then let him settle into his pace. He jumped cleanly, flicking his flaxen tail into the air as he cleared the jump, and I steadied him and turned towards the big rustic oxer. Lucas approached it confidently, his stride smooth and even, until we were only two strides away from the jump. It happened too quickly for me to tell if it was a slip, or a stumble, or simply a misstep, but I felt his rhythm break, one of his forelegs buckled slightly, and his head lowered as he tried to regain his footing. I sat tight and pushed him on, knowing that we could still make it if he recovered in time. We still had time. We still had room. I tried not to think about what had happened to Sam, tried not to review the image of her horse catapulting through the air and landing on top of her.

We can do this, I told myself, clicking my tongue encouragingly to Lucas, who made a valiant effort to correct himself on the last stride. He still felt a little uneven, but he had his head up and his eyes focused on the fence ahead. He was back on the job, and as I squeezed his sides with my lower leg, he took a bold leap over the fence.

"Good boy!" I told him as he jumped, and I saw an ear flicker back towards me in mid-air.

We landed, and he cantered on. His stride was disunited, and I gave him a sharp kick with my inside leg as we rode the bending line, asking for a flying change. He attempted it, stumbled, then righted himself again.

What is up with you? I wondered. He was still cross-cantering, but the vertical fence was only three strides away now, so there was no time to worry about that. It was a long three strides, and I pushed him on for it but Lucas resisted, backing off. That was weird for him, and I clicked my tongue again. *C'mon Lukey!*

He made it to the fence in a short four, and had to jump right off his hocks from the base. I clung tight as he scraped over the top of the high vertical, and my heart sank as I heard his hooves rattle against wood, then the thud of the rail coming down behind us. *Damn!*

But my disappointment at the four faults quickly went out the window as Lucas continued cantering, because there was no mistaking it now. He was lame. I quickly drew him back to a trot, and he limped heavily, his head bobbing with each stride. I jumped to the ground before he'd even made it back to a walk, and Lucas came to a shaky halt beside me, immediately taking the weight off his right foreleg.

Oh no. No no no. Please be okay! I could see Mum from the

corner of my eye, dashing towards me as I pulled the tendon boot off and ran my hand down Lucas's leg, and my blood turned cold as I felt the thick swelling running right along his tendon.

"The good news is, it's only the ligament that he's damaged."

I looked at the vet in hopeful disbelief. "It's not the tendon?"

He shook his head, and I breathed out a relieved sigh.

"That *is* good news," Mum agreed. "Although it's still a long road to recovery."

James nodded, closing the ultrasound machine and standing up. "You know the story," he said, and we did. Molly had done the same thing last season, although she'd somehow managed to injure herself just by running around in the paddock. James went over the details for us again, just in case we'd somehow forgotten the long and arduous rehab required.

"Six weeks of confinement, minimum. We'll rescan him then, and if it looks okay you can start walking him out for ten minutes a day. Straight lines only, and *only* walking." He looked at me sternly, as though I was going to get overexcited and try to work my pony before he was fit. What kind of rider did he think I was? "Four weeks of walking, then if there's no apparent lameness or swelling, he can start slow work in trot. No more than twenty metres at a time, building up over the following four weeks."

His voice droned on, but I was ignoring him now as I frantically calculated what that meant. It was already October. Six weeks of confinement would take us to the start of December. Lucas wouldn't be allowed to trot until January, and there was no chance of cantering or jumping until at least February. *Goodbye season,* I thought sadly, rubbing Lucas's broad white forehead. How had this happened to us again? My season on Molly had been wiped out last year, and now it was apparently Lucas's turn.

The chestnut gelding pushed his face against my chest, wanting to be comforted, and I obliged. It wasn't his fault. If only I'd pulled him up sooner. If only I'd realised what had gone wrong, and hadn't kept going. Mum had told me the whole way home that it wasn't my fault, and how was I to have known, and that even from where she'd been standing he'd looked unbalanced but not lame. I hadn't believed her. I knew it was my fault, and I wasn't sure how I was going to forgive myself.

I looked over at Molly, standing in the next-door stable lipping dreamily at her bucket of feed. *It's all on you now,* I thought, and she lifted her head and looked at me. *It has to be you.*

My bedroom door creaked open, and Mum stuck her head through. "Phone for you."

I groaned as I propped myself up onto my elbows. "I'm trying to sleep."

"It's Steph," she said, and I was instantly awake. "She wants to talk to you."

Mum tossed the cordless phone in my direction, and I grabbed it off the bedspread and lifted it to my ears as she hovered in the doorway, eavesdropping as usual.

"Hello?"

"Hi Katy. I heard about Lucas. He doing okay?"

"Yeah, I think so. He's had some bute so he's feeling better, and the vet thinks he'll make a full recovery," I told her, trying to sound positive.

Why is she asking me about Lucas? She doesn't even own him. Lucas belonged to her best friend, but I'd already spoken with Abby at length about the injury, and she'd been assured that we were doing everything humanly possible to give her pony the best chance of recovery.

"That's good. We need to talk about Molly."

I felt a shiver of trepidation run through me at Steph's words. I wondered if she was mad at me for leaving the show without riding Molly's jump off. I'd been too upset about Lucas's injury to go back out, and I wouldn't have given Molly a good ride even if I had attempted it. The sensitive mare would've picked up immediately on my tension, and most likely wouldn't even have made it over the first jump.

"She's going to be my number one priority from now on," I told Steph quickly. "We're selling some of the other ones, and I'll be focusing on her…"

She cut me off. "Don't bother. We're putting her on the market."

I couldn't breathe. Couldn't speak. Couldn't do anything except sit there as Steph kept talking about selling the pony that had changed my life, and knowing that there wasn't a thing in the world I could do to stop her. I caught snippets of the conversation through the whirl of my thoughts. *Need the money. Sam's hospital bills. Ongoing costs. Interested buyer…*

My brain snapped back into gear at those words, and

I managed to choke out a question. "You've got someone interested?"

"Yes," Steph told me dispassionately. "Susannah Andrews wants to buy her. They're going to take her on trial next week."

3
CRUSH

"How long now until Molly goes?"

I shut the door of Lucas's box and double-checked the latch, then turned to AJ with a sigh. "Three more days. They're picking her up at the show this weekend."

My friend gave me a sympathetic look as she buckled Squib's neckrug. "It's so unfair."

I kicked at a stone in the driveway, watching it bounce across the dirt towards the house. "You're telling me."

"Are you sure you can't convince Steph to sell Molly to you?" AJ asked hopefully, untying Squib's lead rope and preparing to take him out to the paddock. "I mean, she knows that you'll give her an amazing home. Doesn't that count for something?"

"Probably not," I muttered. "It's all about the money right now. I know that they need it, but surely Steph could sell some of *her* horses instead. They're worth way more than Moll."

"Maybe she is," AJ offered. "And you just don't know about it yet."

I shrugged. "Maybe."

The thought had crossed my mind, but I didn't want to entertain it. It was easier to stay mad at Steph if I could believe that she was being selfish, holding onto her own horses while selling the ones she didn't care about anymore. *Wouldn't you?* asked the voice in my head, but I squashed it down and ignored it.

AJ gave me a pat on the shoulder as she led her pony past, and I stood with my back to the stables and watched them go. Squib strode forward purposefully, and AJ walked at his shoulder, then slung an arm over his withers and gave him a pat, as though reassuring herself that he was all hers, and always would be.

Lucky her.

My head turned as I heard a car approaching up the driveway, and I turned to see a dark green sedan pull in, loud music thumping out through the open windows. Instinctively I stood up straighter and brushed as much of the hay and dirt off my jodhpurs as I could. The car parked up next to the stables, and Anders opened the driver's door and swung his long legs onto the ground.

AJ would never admit it, but her brother was gorgeous. At seventeen, he was tall with golden hair that somehow got darker in the sun, and intense grey-blue eyes. When he smiled, he got a dimple in his left cheek, and I got ten thousand butterflies in my stomach. I first noticed him at school last year, when he was presented with some award at assembly. I'd been sitting in the auditorium, half asleep with boredom and thinking about my ponies, when he'd walked across the stage in front of me and I swear I'd almost died. I'd committed his name to memory as the award was handed to him, and had even gone out of my way a couple of times to cross his path in the hallways at school. He'd never noticed me, of course. Just another nameless, faceless student, two years younger than him and completely off his radar. But a few weeks ago I'd met AJ and we'd quickly become friends. Of course, I had no idea when I first met her that Anders Maclean was her brother, but it definitely came as an added bonus to her friendship.

"Hey Katy." Anders unfolded himself from the car and stretched, his t-shirt riding up to reveal a small patch of flat, bare stomach.

"Hi." I tried to sound casual, friendly but not over-excited. I'd still only spoken to him a couple of times, and hearing him say my name was enough to have my stomach doing somersaults.

"AJ around?"

"Um, she's just turning Squib out."

I shifted my weight onto my other foot, trying to think of something interesting or cool to say. Lucas stuck his head over the door of his box and snorted, spraying me with bits of feed, snot and saliva.

Embarrassed, I wiped at my cheek. "Ugh, Lucas. Do you have to?"

Anders laughed, and came closer to us. I could feel my heart rate increasing rapidly as he walked up to my pony and held a hand out to him.

"Is he friendly?"

"Sure." Lucas lipped hopefully around on Anders's palm, then licked him just to be sure. "He's hoping you have carrots."

Anders looked directly at me, and I wondered how my knees were actually still holding me up. "Sorry to disappoint him."

I shrugged. "He'll live."

Lucas took his cue to look disgusted with us both, and wandered back to his hay as Anders leaned on the front of the box and looked in at Lucas's rucked-up bedding.

"How come he's not out in the paddock?"

"He's injured."

"Bugger. Will he be okay?"

The concerned look on Anders's face was enough to have my insides humming again, just as I'd started to calm them down. I folded my arms across my chest, then wondered if that made me look defensive and uncrossed them again.

"Eventually," I told Anders. "But he's got to stay in there for the next three months, give or take."

"No way! What'd he do?"

"Tore a ligament." I didn't want him to ask how it happened, so I changed the subject. "Here's AJ."

Anders turned to see his sister approaching, and straightened up, making me regret drawing his attention away from me.

"About time," he called to her.

AJ checked her watch and shook her head emphatically. "Not even. You're early."

"I'm never early," Anders replied easily, then shot a grin at me that just about swept my legs out from under me, before looking back over at his sister. "You should know that by now."

"Whatever." AJ was wholly unaffected by her brother's charm. "I'll just put Squib's gear away, then you can drag me home."

"Kicking and screaming, no doubt," Anders said, and leaned against the wall again, turning back towards me. "She loves it here."

"Thanks," I said, then immediately wanted to kick myself. *Thanks?*

Luckily for me, Anders didn't seem to notice that it was a weird thing to say. Either that or he was too polite to blatantly laugh at me. He just looked around, his smoky blue eyes taking in everything, and I wondered what he was seeing. I tried to see our farm as a stranger might. The big five-bay shed that we were standing in, which had been machinery storage when we moved here but was now three looseboxes, a tack room and a hay barn. The small house, its paint peeling around the windows and door frames, with discarded boots and old covers and firewood piled haphazardly by the door. The small arena with its shabby homemade jumps, surrounded by flax bushes and willow trees and lichen-covered post and rail fences. It wasn't big and it wasn't flash, but it suited us fine.

"Okay, I'm ready."

AJ walked back up to us, pulling her jacket on. The sun had gone down and although the days were getting warmer, it was still only October, and summer wasn't quite upon us yet.

"I hope you've got some money on you," Anders told her. "Because Mum's working and Dad's out, so we have to get our own dinner."

AJ scowled at him. "Since when do I ever have any money? You're the one with a job."

"Yeah, but I don't have enough to buy *you* dinner," Anders replied. "Not with the amount you eat. I'll go broke."

"Shut up." AJ kicked her brother in the side of the leg, and Anders reacted fast, swiping her ankle out and then putting her into a headlock. She squirmed, but he held her fast.

"What was that?" he teased.

"I said shut up," AJ repeated defiantly.

Anders looked at me. "She's a slow learner, this one."

The porch lights flicked on, and I glanced at our house. "You guys can stay here for dinner, if you want."

Anders released his hold on AJ, who straightened up immediately and aimed another kick at him.

"Careful," he warned her. "Or you'll be walking home." He turned back to me. "Thanks for the offer, but Poss and I would eat you out of house and home."

I'd forgotten about AJ's nickname, and it took me a moment to realise who he meant, but I quickly shook my head.

"Mum's made heaps," I told him, and it was true. I'd seen her that afternoon cutting up vegetables for a huge pot of stew. I also knew that it was supposed to last us two or three nights, but she wouldn't object if I brought them in to share. "Seriously. Come on, I'll ask."

Anders hung back, but AJ stepped up next to me and hooked her arm through mine. "Sounds a lot better than Pizza Hut."

"I cannot understand how a sister of mine doesn't like pizza," Anders muttered as he followed us somewhat reluctantly over to the house.

"I like pizza," AJ retorted. "Just not sponges or cardboard, and that's what their pizzas taste like."

Her brother rolled his eyes as we stepped up onto the porch, and I threw the door open. The smell of Mum's stew came flowing towards us, and I heard Anders's stomach rumble. I unzipped my chaps and grinned at him.

"Hungry?"

"Maybe a bit. You sure your mum won't mind?"

"Course not. Mum!" I yelled as I kicked my boots off and walked into the house. "AJ and her brother are staying for dinner. That's okay, right?"

Mum looked surprised as the three of us came into the kitchen. AJ sat down at the table, feeling right at home, but Anders lingered in the doorway.

"Only if you can spare it," he insisted, giving Mum his most disarming smile. "We can always grab some takeaways on the way home if you don't have enough."

I took one look at Mum's face, and I knew that she was sold. Immediately charmed, she gestured Anders towards the table with a wooden spoon, dripping gravy on the floor which Critter immediately licked up.

"Of course, come on in. I've made heaps. It's nice to meet you," she added. "Anders, I presume."

"That's me."

He took two steps towards her and held out his hand to her. I watched my mother accept his handshake, wondering what his fingers felt like, whether his palm was rough or smooth. Wishing he was making that kind of intense eye contact with me instead.

"Well. Lovely to meet you."

Mum sounded slightly flustered, as though she was crushing on Anders herself, and I wanted to shake her. *Gross.*

"Who's thirsty?" I asked loudly, walking towards the fridge and forcing Mum to retract her hand from Anders's as I pushed through between them. "We've got apple juice, and…" I pulled the large plastic juice container out of the fridge and looked at the brown sludgy remains at the bottom. "Or not. We have water."

"Water's fine, thanks." Anders sat down at the kitchen table opposite his sister, who was leafing through a recent issue of the Bulletin and ignoring him. I filled the glasses with tap water, wondering whether to add ice or not, as she flipped the page.

"This is a good photo."

I glanced over her shoulder as I carried the drinks back to the table and set them down. "Yeah, except for my lower leg."

"There's nothing wrong with your lower leg," AJ lied, and my face flushed as Anders leaned over to get a look at the picture in the magazine.

It was of me and Lucas in the Grand Prix at Te Teko, and it was a pretty cool shot. Taken side-on as we jumped a big airy oxer, Lucas had all four feet tucked up underneath him, and aside from the fact that my lower leg had slid half a mile back behind the girth, it looked impressive.

Anders glanced up at me. "That's you?"

"Yeah." I filled my own water glass and sat down at the table. I wanted to sit next to him, but I thought it might seem weird or obvious, so I took the seat on the other side of AJ.

"That jump's huge!"

"It's not that big," I shrugged. "Only a two-star."

"Bigger than AJ can jump." She elbowed him indignantly, but he gave her a knowing look. "Well, it is!"

"Give me time."

Anders's eyes flickered back to me. "So did you win?"

"Yeah." My fleeting moment of pride was quickly subdued as I thought of Lucas standing in his box, trapped in there for months of rehab. "Not that it matters now."

"Someone set the table please," Mum said as she started pulling bowls out of the cupboard.

AJ got to her feet, leaving the magazine splayed out on the table. Anders and I both reached for it at the same time, then both pulled our hands away simultaneously. He laughed, and pushed the magazine towards me slightly.

"You have it."

"I've already read it," I admitted. "I was just going to put it away. But you can read it, if you want." I felt my skin redden again. *Why would he want to read it?*

"Do you have any interest in horses, Anders?" Mum asked him, saving me.

"Not really," he admitted as AJ dumped a handful of cutlery onto the table.

I grabbed the magazine out of the way and threw it onto the bench. At least, I tried to throw it onto the bench, but it missed and fell into Critter's bed, half-landing on him and making him leap up with a yelp.

"Sorry Crit," I told him as I picked him up and gave him a cuddle. He licked my chin, and I scruffed his head, then glanced at Anders, who was watching me with his eyebrows raised. "What?"

"You call that a dog?"

"Just because your dog is a giant," I retorted. AJ's family had a retired police dog, presumably because their mother was a detective, and he was a huge German Shepherd with a loud bark but a squishy personality once he got to know you. "What would you call him, then?"

"House rat," Anders grinned, then turned to smile at Mum as she put a big bowl of stew down in front of him. "This looks amazing, thanks so much."

Mum beamed at him. She was still falling for his charm, and it was starting to feel a bit creepy.

"Oh, it's no problem at all. I made far too much for the two of us anyway, so you're doing us a favour."

She grabbed a loaf of sliced white bread out of the pantry and set it on the table as well. I hoped it wasn't stale, but I had a suspicion it'd been in there for a few days. I certainly wasn't eating it, and I watched uncomfortably as Anders helped himself to a slice.

"Eat up," Mum commanded as she set bowls of stew down in front of me and AJ.

We picked up our spoons obediently as she dished out her own bowl, but Anders politely waited for Mum to be sitting down before he started eating. If the bread was stale, he didn't mention it. Mum chatted with him as we ate, which turned out to be not as awkward as I'd imagined, because she asked all kinds of questions that I would've been too shy to ask, and he answered them all honestly. Through their conversation, I learned that he played at fullback for our school's First XV rugby team, and was considered likely to captain the team next year; that his favourite subject was Graphic Design and his least favourite was English; and that he wanted to be an architect when he left school, but he wasn't sure whether he'd go straight to university or take a gap year and travel around Europe. At that point, Mum had launched into stories of her own travels, which she'd undertaken right after leaving school. Like him, she'd planned to take a year off and see some of the world before heading to uni, but she'd become addicted to travelling and hadn't returned home until she ran out of money.

"I'd been having far too much fun overseas to consider sitting in a lecture theatre for the next three years, so I got a job and started saving to go back again. Not that I ever made it," Mum said with a heavy sigh.

"What happened?" Anders asked as I glared across the table at my mother.

"Katy did," she told him. "I fell pregnant, and that was that."

"Try not to make it sound like the worst thing that ever happened to you," I muttered.

"Of course it's not, darling," Mum said quickly. "You're the best thing that ever happened to me, you know that." She shovelled another spoonful of stew into her mouth and chewed, then swallowed. "Would've been nice to get to Nepal, though. That was next on my list."

Out of the corner of my eye, I could see Anders looking at me, but I concentrated on my meal until he looked away, turning back to my mother.

"So you never made it to uni, huh? What were you planning on studying?"

"Fine Arts," Mum admitted, rolling her eyes at herself. "Not exactly a money spinner."

Anders shrugged. "More to life than money," he replied easily.

I kept my eyes on my food. *Easy to say when you've got plenty of it,* I thought, then felt bad. I'd been to their house and I knew that they didn't have a lot of spare change lying around. Their sister Alexia had Asperger's Syndrome, and according to AJ, her parents had spent a lot of money over the years getting Alexia into extra tutoring and other programmes to try and help her. I didn't like Alexia much. She was hard to talk to, abrasive and downright rude sometimes, and I didn't really know how to act around her. Luckily AJ preferred my house to hers, so we spent most of our time together here.

"That was amazing," Anders said, putting his spoon down and smiling at Mum. "I'd ask for the recipe, but I bet nobody can make it like you."

"You're such a greaser," AJ scolded him, then smiled at Mum as she scraped her own plate. "It *was* delicious though. If you ever make it again, I'll be in here like a shot."

"I'm just glad to have such appreciative diners," Mum replied, looking at my bowl which was still half-full. Everyone's eyes followed her, making me self-conscious.

"You gave me too much," I told her. "I can't eat it all."

"Anders'll finish it," AJ told me. "He's like a garbage disposal. Between him and Aidan, there's never any leftovers at our house. Probably why we eat so fast," she added, looking at her and her brother's empty bowls guiltily. "More out of necessity than greed, I promise."

"He can if he wants." I laid my spoon down and pushed the bowl towards Anders. "I'm done."

"Sure? You've hardly eaten anything," he said, even as he picked up his spoon.

"I'll have a snack later if I get hungry," I told him.

Mum shook her head at me. "Eats like a sparrow, this one. Constantly snacking, but its a waste of time to take her out for a meal because she'll only pick at it. She's always been that way."

"I hate feeling full," I said, shuddering as I tried to explain. "Ugh. It's horrible."

Anders shook his head at me as he started to eat my dinner. "You're a weird one, Katy-did. No wonder you're friends with my sister."

"He's a nice young man," Mum said as she stacked the dishwasher and I came back into the room after watching Anders's headlights disappear down our driveway.

"Yep."

"Good-looking, too."

"Mum!"

"What? I'm forty, not blind."

I shuddered as I cleared the table. "Gross."

"Not the adjective I'd have chosen," Mum teased, and I pulled a face at her, then dumped the plates on the bench.

"I'm going to do my homework."

"Okay." She let me get halfway across the room before she spoke again. "Katy?"

"Yeah?"

"Be careful, okay?"

"Huh?"

"He's AJ's brother. I'd hate to see something come between you two. Especially a boy."

"Oh my God. I *know* he's AJ's brother, I'm not stupid."

"I know you're not." Mum was facing me now. "But you're young still, and there's a lot you don't know about…"

I cut her off before she could go somewhere super uncomfortable. "I'm fifteen, not five. And I *know* all this. Just leave it, okay? It's not even like that."

And I left the room before she could say anything else.

4

BETRAYAL

The best thing about competing at the Hawke's Bay show grounds was their proximity to home. I got up at the highly civilised hour of seven-thirty on Friday morning and loaded the ponies, kissed Lucas goodbye, and gave Puppet a scratch too. He was shut into the loosebox next to Lucas to keep him company, and he was happily pulling at his stuffed haynet while Lucas paced around in agitation at being left behind.

"Sorry buddy." We lifted the truck ramp and I heard Molly whinny back to him. I tried not to think about what it was going to be like to come home without her. "We'll be back tonight, I promise. And Hannah will bring you some lunch."

Hannah was the oldest of the Fitzherbert kids, our friends who lived down the road, and was home from uni on a study break. She'd promised Mum that she would to look in on the ponies during the day, make sure they hadn't come to any harm while we were gone.

Lucas wasn't reassured, and he called out and banged on his stall door as we started the truck. I watched him turn fuzzy through unshed tears as Mum backed the truck out and headed down the driveway, leaving him behind.

I pulled Molly's forelegs forward to smooth out the wrinkles under her wide stud girth, then gave her glossy neck a rub. I hadn't seen any sign of Steph since we'd arrived, or of Susannah. Mum had made noises about going and seeking them out, but I'd quickly dissuaded her. I took Molly's reins and prepared to lead her out of her yard when I heard voices approaching, and stopped, my heart plummeting into my stomach.

Susannah and her parents were striding towards us, and as happy as I'd have been to completely ignore them, Steph was with them, so I had no choice but to stand there and watch them approach. The smiles on their faces widened as they looked at Molly, standing fit and proud behind me.

Steph reached me first, and I swallowed hard.

"Hi Katy. She's looking good."

I couldn't speak. I didn't want to look at them, let alone talk to them, and I wondered where on earth Mum had got to. Steph's hand reached out towards Molly's reins, and I let her take them away from me.

"Susannah's going to take her around the metre-fifteen," she told me heartlessly. "It'll be a good chance for her to get a feel for her in the ring. She's a straightforward ride at home, but she can be a different creature when she's competing."

Steph smiled at Susannah, making light of the fact that she'd never been able to get the pony to perform, and that she'd written her off as a lost cause until I'd come along and proven her worth. Until I'd made her into a pony worth selling. But there was no guarantee that Susannah would be able to get her to jump either. Maybe this was the best way. Maybe Molly would refuse in the ring, and Susannah would fall off, and Steph would apologise to me for even thinking of taking my pony away because she was a real one-person pony and would never perform for anyone else. And then she'd admit defeat and give her to me to keep forever. I clung onto those hopes as I watched Susannah step forward and give Molly a gentle pat, then walk alongside her as Steph led the mare down towards the jumping rings.

And then when they were gone, I turned away and let myself cry.

Forbes strained against the lead rope, tugging me towards more grass. I let him pull me along, ignoring my mother's voice in my head, telling me to demand his respect and establish my own personal space. If Forbes wanted that particular patch of long grass over there, he could have it. I was done arguing.

Robin followed willingly, as placid as always about whatever life threw at him. I hadn't wanted to stand around on my own at the yards, and Mum was still nowhere to be seen, so I had taken the boys for a walk and a pick of grass. I'd purposely left my cell phone in the truck. If Mum came back and wondered where I was, she was going to have to come and find me. But now I was wondering if AJ had texted me, and when she was going to get here. Her parents didn't like her skipping school, and she'd had to work hard to convince them to let her even have this afternoon off. It had never bothered Mum to give me time off school, as long as I kept up with my homework and assignments, which for the most part, I did. Squib hadn't been too pleased when I'd taken his friends away, and had been whinnying and running around his yard when I left, but there were other ponies just over the railing from him, so it wasn't like he was totally alone.

I was starting to regret bringing both the boys out at once though. Forbes was still bolshy on the lead, and he kept aiming kicks at Robin, warning him to stay out of his space and making Robin pull back to the end of the lead with his legs braced, yanking my arm almost out of its socket repeatedly.

After fifteen minutes of being pulled in one direction and then the other by my recalcitrant ponies, my mood was only getting worse, so I started walking them back. Robin marched alongside me as Forbes dragged back, unwilling to leave the world's tastiest grass that he'd just discovered by the fence. He still had long strands of it hanging from his mouth, and I watched him chew as he followed me sulkily back across the show grounds.

"At least you're good looking," I told him, and he snorted at me.

It was true though. Despite being a plain dark bay with barely any white on him, Forbes was a head-turner. His conformation was almost flawless, and his curved ears and slightly dished face made for a very attractive picture. He was fairly well-bred too, an undersized Warmblood-Thoroughbred cross that had been bred for jumping. We'd bought him cheap and unbroken, because he'd been a bit of an ugly duckling, but after a couple of years turned out on the hills, he'd grown into himself. He had plenty of natural jumping ability, but he also had a stubborn streak a mile wide. We'd already had a couple of arguments, but so far I'd managed to win them all through quiet perseverance.

But the big battle was still coming, I could tell. Someday I was going to ask him to do something he *really* didn't want to do, and I was going to have to win. I wasn't looking forward to that day.

We were almost back at the yards when I saw Susannah. She was still in the warm-up, cantering Molly in a circle. My pony was flexed and on the bit, soft in the hand and working through her body correctly. Steph was standing by the practice fence, calling instructions, and I watched as Susannah cantered towards the jump. It was an oxer, set high and wide and square across - Molly's least favourite kind of jump. She'd jump verticals all day long, but oxers took a bit more leg and a steadier hand. I stopped in my tracks and watched Molly canter down to the fence. Her head lifted slightly and I saw her fall back behind Susannah's leg. Steph called something to her, Susannah rode forward a touch more, and Molly soared cleanly over with her ears pricked forward.

I was grooming Forbes when Susannah brought Molly back. Mum was walking behind her, chatting to Susannah's father as though they were long-lost friends. *So that's where she'd disappeared off to.* I ran the body brush over Forbes's rounded hindquarters once more, then looked up reluctantly as Susannah stopped in front of his yard.

"Where should I put her?"

Forbes reached over the railing and sniffed at Molly, who squealed at him and laid her ears flat back, making Susannah jump. I motioned to the yard next to Forbes with my brush.

"In there's fine. I'll untack her."

"I can do it." She led Molly into the yard and hitched up the gate as I ducked through the railings between them.

"I've got it." I unbuckled Molly's girth swiftly. "I need the saddle anyway, for Forbes."

That wasn't even true – Forbes had his own saddle. I don't know why I lied, or why Susannah's very presence seemed to bring out the worst in me.

I pulled the saddle off Molly's back and slung it over the divider as Susannah continued to ignore my request to let me deal with my own pony, and slipped Molly's bridle off. Molly lifted her head a bit as she did, and the bit clanked against her teeth, startling her.

"I said to let me do that," I snapped at Susannah as I rubbed Molly's sweaty neck reassuringly. She was damp and still blowing slightly, and would need a thorough wash and a long walk to ease her tight muscles. "You have to take her bridle off really slowly and let her drop the bit on her own."

Susannah met my eyes with her own icy stare. "Well I didn't know that, did I?"

"It's called common sense," I replied. "And it's how you should unbridle any pony."

Susannah opened her mouth to retort when her father came to the front of the yard. "Susie, we have to go."

Susannah glanced back at Molly, slick with sweat, the veins still popping out against her skin.

"She'll need cooling off," she told me, as though I had no idea how to look after a pony.

That was the pot calling the kettle black if ever I'd heard it, and I would've told her so except that she had at least enough common sense to get out of there before I had time to reply.

I grabbed a sponge bucket and got to work on Molly as Mum said goodbye to Susannah and her father, shaking their hands and smiling as though they were lovely people who would give Molly a top home, not vile people who would probably tie her head to her chest and beat her senseless if she didn't perform for them. I closed my eyes and laid my head against Molly's damp neck, fighting back tears.

"You probably don't want to hear it, but she went well for her."

Of course I don't want to hear it, I wanted to yell. "I hate her."

"I know."

I lifted my head and looked at my mother. "She'll be horrible to her."

Mum looked unconvinced. "She's riding a lot better these days."

"In public," I agreed. "She has to. She could hardly come back out and ride the way she used to after everything that happened. But what about behind closed doors? What's going on there?"

Mum sighed, knowing I was right. "The decision isn't up to us."

"Oh really? Wow I had no idea."

I grabbed Molly's halter and buckled it onto her head. She rolled her eyes uneasily at me, but I was in too much of a hurry to care. I picked up her trailing lead rope and opened the gate, leading her out into the aisle. Mum said something, but I ignored her, marching out of the yards and back to the far corner of the grounds where Forbes had found that wonderfully delicious patch of grass. I wanted Molly to have it.

"There you are."

Mum came up behind me as I watched Molly tuck into the long green stuff. She was carrying a sweat sheet over her arm and she threw it over Molly's back, protecting her from the cool breeze that was making goosebumps form on my arms.

"If you're going to tell me to stop acting like a spoiled brat, you can save your breath," I told her.

"I wasn't going to say anything of the sort." Mum put her arms around me and pulled me in close. "I'm so sorry. I wish we could keep her. You know I do."

I nodded, burying my face in Mum's bony shoulder. "I know."

"I would buy her for you if I could."

"I know you would." I took a shaky breath, thinking hard. "We should've planned for this. Kept some money in reserve, in case this happened."

"What money?" Mum asked reasonably. "Everything that comes in goes out, you know that."

"We should've have let Fossick go so cheaply."

"It was the right home," Mum argued, but I snorted.

"Mounted games? The way that pony could jump? Pull the other one. We should've held out for someone who wanted to show jump her. Kept her a bit longer, got her really going at a metre ten…"

"Katy." There was a warning in Mum's voice that I chose to ignore.

"What if we sell everything else? If Robin wins this afternoon, he could fetch a decent price. If we market him as a show hunter instead of a Pony Club plodder, he'd be worth way more."

"We can try that," Mum agreed, giving me a last squeeze before she let me go. "Now you'd better get back and get Forbes tacked up, because his class is about to start. They were walking it when I came over here. I'll stay with Moll, keep cooling her out."

I looked at Molly, contentedly cropping the grass and blissfully unaware of her impending doom. "Why couldn't you have been naughty?" I asked her. "Why'd you have to be so good?"

I didn't get an answer, so I passed her lead rope to Mum and walked back to the yards, wondering if there was any possible way to change the course of fate.

Forbes jumped well, but sucked back behind my leg at the double and had a rail down. I rode him back to the yards on a loose rein, my feet dangling next to the stirrups, to discover that AJ had finally arrived. She was leaning over Squib's yard railing, rubbing his forehead and feeding him peppermints.

"You'll rot his teeth," I told her as I jumped to the ground and led Forbes into his yard.

"I'm not feeding him *that* many," she replied cheerfully. "How'd Forbesy go?"

"One down in the first round. When did you get here?"

"About three minutes ago. Anders brought me up."

I glanced around. "Is he still here?"

AJ gave me a weird look. "He dropped me at the gate."

"Oh." I could sense that she wanted to say something else, so I quickly changed the subject. "Well, Susannah rode Molly this morning, and the little traitor jumped double clear."

"That's a shame," AJ commiserated. "But at least you know she'll be happy, if she goes to them."

I unbuckled the girth and lifted the saddle off Forbes's back. "Doubtful. I don't see how any pony could be happy, belonging to her."

"She's not that bad," AJ said, and I shot her a look.

"Excuse me?"

"Susannah. She's not that bad."

I scoffed. "What would you know about it? You don't even know her."

AJ shrugged. "I just don't think she's as horrible as you make her out to be."

"I *told* you what she did. And you want to be friends with her? You think I should sell my pony to her?"

"I didn't say I wanted to be friends with her. I just said that I don't think she's all that bad. And if Molly likes her, then that's got to be a good thing, right? I mean, you wouldn't want Molly to go to someone who can't ride her. You wouldn't want to see her going badly."

Wouldn't I? I wouldn't want to see her unhappy, but I hadn't realised how much of my own pride and sense of self-worth had come from my achievements with Molly until they'd started to be ripped away from me.

"I don't want her to go to Susannah."

"Well, you don't really have a choice, do you?" AJ asked, her voice starting to carry. "You said yourself that you can't afford the pony, so someone has to buy her, and you might as well be friends with that person."

She turned to walk away, but I couldn't let her leave it at that. "So I should just stand back while she's sold to a family with a criminal conviction for horse abuse?" I snapped. "Susannah might've fooled you and a few other people, but she hasn't changed. You just wait and see."

AJ turned back to me, her expression unreadable. "You told me yourself that the girl whose pony was attacked has forgiven Susannah. Why can't you?"

I hesitated, trying to find the right words to explain that forgiveness was not something you just handed out because other people were saintly or naïve. But AJ wasn't done.

"You're carrying around someone else's baggage, Katy. For Molly's sake, and for your own, you have to let it go."

That was easy for her to say, but she wasn't there when it all went down. Hadn't seen the aftermath, couldn't possibly understand just how horrific the whole ordeal had been. Not just for the victim and her family, who of course had been the worst affected, but for all of us. The very thought that someone was capable of sabotaging another rider's efforts to win, just so that they would have a better chance themselves, had shocked everyone. I'd seen the scars that the attack had left behind on the innocent pony who'd been caught in the middle of it all. The whole incident was sickening, and had no place in our sport. At least not the version of it that I knew.

I pushed the thoughts out of my mind as I trotted Robin across the show hunter arena, and asked him to pick up a canter. He resisted slightly, then made a jerky upward transition. I should've taken more time over his warm-up, but I'd miscalculated the length of time it would take to get AJ and the sugar-high Squib prepped for their class. We'd put our fight behind us, and as their self-appointed coach, their success mattered to me, and a good warm-up was crucial to get Squib focused in the ring. It'd worked, too. AJ's chunky grey pony had been full of himself as usual, but he'd jumped a super clear round in the metre-ten speed, just slightly too slow to finish in the ribbons.

By the time we'd waited for the results and congratulated the winners, then walked back to the yards, I'd found Mum frantically dragging a fully-tacked Robin over towards the show hunters, yelling at me to hurry up and get dressed and get on my pony. I'd only been in the saddle for a few minutes, and a quick canter on each rein was all I'd managed to do to warm him up. Luckily the jumps were only small, and it was hardly going to tax him to canter slowly over them.

I aimed him towards the first fence, and he jumped it cleanly. Cantered around the corner, made a wide, sweeping turn to fence two, and cantered a steady five strides down to fence three. Robin popped calmly over, but he was lazy behind and I heard his hooves rattle the back rail. That would knock points off his score, and I dug my spurs into his side a little as we cantered the turn. He responded by picking up his pace slightly, and took the brush fence well out of a bold stride. He pecked a bit on landing though, and I had to slip my reins a fraction to let him regain his balance. Fortunately we still had four strides to reach the next jump, but he was lazy off the ground, and tapped the front rail. I wanted to growl at him, but we were cantering right past the judge, so I kept my irritation to myself and rode Robin on around the turn.

He was on the wrong lead, so I asked him for a flying change. He resisted, and I was forced to click my tongue at him and use my spur firmly to get him to respond. Robin skipped a little and changed behind, but was still wrong in front. It was too late now to change it, as we were only a handful of strides from the last three fences, so I was forced to accept that we'd cross-cantered the corner.

No ribbons for you today, I thought at Robin as he jumped over the low wall. *Lazy sod.* He landed smoothly, took four even strides and jumped over the white rails of the oxer. Two strides and he was out over the last fence, and I brought him back to a trot and headed him towards the gate.

Mum was standing there, frowning at me as we approached. Probably about to lambast me for a terrible round, which I knew I'd had so there was no reason for her to rub it in. But as the next rider came into the ring, I suddenly felt what she'd clearly noticed. A hitch in Robin's stride. I slowed his trot more, and it became more pronounced until there was no longer any doubt in either of our minds.

Robin was lame.

5

TEMPTATION

"Do you know what's wrong with him?"

I shook my head at AJ the next morning as I tightened Molly's girth. We'd arrived back at the show grounds for the second day of competition, and after getting the ponies off the truck – minus Robin, who had now taken over Puppet's babysitting duties in the box stall next to Lucas – I wanted nothing more than to get into the saddle and just ride.

"Hard to tell. There's no major heat or swelling, other than some heel pain. Mum's going to get the vet in to take a look at him, since he's no better this morning."

"Who's not better?"

Hayley Maxwell came strolling down the aisle towards us, and AJ pulled a face and turned away from her, returning her attentions to Squib, who was leaning over his railing and shoving his upper lip at her, trying to persuade her to give him more of his beloved peppermints. Hayley stopped front of me and leaned against Molly's yard.

"Robin. He went lame yesterday."

I lifted Molly's bridle to her head and slipped it on, then buckled the throatlash.

"Not another one! Man, you're having some bad luck lately," Hayley said, shaking her head at me.

As if I hadn't noticed that my ponies were dropping like flies. I'd barely slept last night, feeling terrible about it, still sure that it was somehow my fault.

Hayley was still talking. "So I don't know if you saw yesterday, but Tess just about killed herself in the Speed class."

I shook my head. "Must've missed it. What happened?"

Hayley groaned. "Same old story. Came out of the corner to the big square oxer and started pulling on Misty's mouth. I yelled at her to let his head go, so what does she do? Drops the contact completely and just grabs a handful of his mane. And of course she didn't have her leg on, so naturally Misty decided to go past the jump instead of over it, and Tess ate dirt. How she managed to fall off while holding the mane is anyone's guess. So I told Mum last night that that's it. She's not riding him anymore, I want him to go on lease. And that's where *you* come in."

I paused, my hands stilling on Molly's noseband. "Really?"

"Absolutely. You'll be able to handle him, and you're short on Grand Prix ponies right now. It's win-win."

I smiled at her, trying not to get my hopes up too high. "Won't your parents just want to sell him?"

Hayley scoffed. "I'd like to see them try. They're not that stupid, they know I'd never forgive them." She shook her long hair out and grinned at me. "What d'you say? Mum still wants Tess to ride him this afternoon, but I'm planning on stealing him away before the class and hiding him somewhere so she can't. He's entered in the Grand Prix tomorrow morning, so

I'll try talk Mum into letting you take him in it as a test run. Sound good?"

"Sounds fantastic," I agreed. "Thanks so much!"

Hayley strode off to get her horse ready for the Junior Rider class, and I led Molly out and swung up into her saddle. AJ gave me a curious look as Squib chewed on her t-shirt.

"You must be on early this morning," she commented. "It's not even eight yet and the ring doesn't open until nine."

"I want to get a proper warm-up," I told her. "After Robin yesterday, I'm paranoid about underdoing it. And it'll be good for her to stretch her legs."

"Fair enough," AJ shrugged and I rode out from under the shaky tin roof and into the open.

It was a beautiful morning, crisp and clear, and Molly jig-jogged slightly as we set off. It felt so good to be on her back again, and I ran a gentle hand down her arched neck. She flinched it away from me, full of high spirits, and I laughed and let her move up into a slow trot, following the dirt road that ran along the side of the rings and down past the stable block. There were a few people up and about, mucking out stables or leading rugged and bandaged horses out for a morning pick of grass. Several said hello to me, and I smiled and waved as we passed them. Steph's truck was parked near the end of the block, and I gritted my teeth as I let Molly trot on more energetically past it. I hadn't been entirely truthful with AJ earlier. Molly didn't need too much of a warm-up – in fact, she usually jumped better with just a short work-in – but I hadn't wanted to risk having Susannah turn up again, demanding to ride her. If I'd done the warm-up, Susannah couldn't take over the ride for the class.

So here I was, in Molly's saddle more than an hour before her class was due to open, because I was too scared to risk missing out on what might be one of the last rides I would ever have on my favourite mare.

Despite my concerns, neither Susannah nor Steph turned up and tried to drag me off Molly. Maybe it was because Steph had seen me riding by that morning, or maybe they just hadn't planned on it. But I was so wired by the prospect, and Molly was so het-up by her prolonged warm-up, that our round in the 1.25m didn't go very well at all. Instead of me proving that Molly loved me most and that I was the best possible rider for her, we had a shocking round, finishing with three rails down and a time fault. I rode out of the ring with my head hanging, feeling decidedly sorry for myself.

AJ was sympathetic, but Mum wasn't. She knew it was my fault for over-working Molly too early, and she told me so. In the end I grabbed AJ and we went for a walk to watch the show ponies, which was more like watching paint dry, but at least I didn't have to listen to Mum railing on about how disappointed she was in me. We sat on the grass and watched the ponies trot around and around in circles, their riders perched stiffly in the saddles, and tried to guess who the winners would be. I was better at it than AJ, but neither of us ever completely agreed with the judge's decision.

At least not until the Working Hunter ponies came in, and a beautiful dark bay mare did a super workout that we couldn't fault. It wasn't until the rider was leaving the ring with a smile on her face that I recognised Tessa Maxwell in the saddle. I'd thought the pony looked familiar - she'd had the reliable bay for several years now. I wondered how Tess felt about Hayley's offer. From what I'd seen of her on-board Misty, and comparing it with how much happier and more relaxed she looked on her own pony, I couldn't imagine her being too upset about losing the ride.

I'd just started to ask AJ what she thought of me riding Misty when her phone rang.

"Hold that thought," she told me, then answered the call with no preamble. "What?"

I raised my eyebrows at her abrupt greeting, and went back to watching the chestnut pony now in the ring. The rider was supposed to be doing a hand gallop, which in showing terms means a bold forward canter, but her pony had interpreted it as an actual gallop, and was on its second lap of the ring with her leaning back and hauling on the reins in a vain attempt to slow him. It didn't work, and moments later the pony had jumped the picket fence that divided the ring from the warm-up area and galloped away.

"Show jumping rings are that way!" I heard someone call, and I laughed as AJ finished her conversation and hung up.

"That was dramatic," she said, her eyes following the chestnut pony as it disappeared into the distance.

"Reckon. Who was that?" I asked, motioning towards the phone she was just shoving back into her pocket.

AJ was frowning slightly as she stood up and brushed herself off. "Anders. He got up late, always dangerous in our house, and discovered that everyone's gone out except Astrid, so he's now officially stuck babysitting her for the day."

"And he rang you to complain about it?" I asked as we walked back towards our yards, wondering if Mum had simmered down yet.

Even if she hadn't, I was going to have to deal with it. Our next class would be starting soon, and Forbes and Squib had to be got ready.

"He rang to see if he could bring her here and leave her with me," AJ clarified. "So of course I said hell no. The last thing we need is Astrid following us around all day."

I shrugged. "Mum'd look after her. She'd probably just sit in our truck and read, wouldn't she?"

Astrid was twelve years old and unlike the rest of AJ's loud, energetic family, she was a bookworm who kept mostly to herself. The couple of times I'd seen her, she'd always had her nose in a book and her iPod plugged into her ears, living in her own imaginary world.

"Maybe. But Anders always gets out of things like that, so I told him he should get up earlier in future and then these things wouldn't happen to him. He's coming up anyway, and dragging Astrid along. Probably to punish her, because wandering around in crowds of people all day is like her worst nightmare, but whatever. It won't kill her."

I filtered through the barrage of information for the important part. "Anders is coming to the show?"

"Yeah. Says he wants to watch Squib jump."

AJ's tone was disparaging, but there was a trace of hopefulness in it too. Her parents had bought her a pony to keep her happy, but they were too busy working and looking after her four siblings to spend much time with her. She'd told me once that her mother hadn't seen her ride Squib since the day they'd bought him. Her brother and sister coming to watch her ride today was a big deal for her, whatever she said, and I slung my arm across her shoulders and gave her an encouraging squeeze.

"Well then. Let's go get him ready to knock their socks off!"

Squib had certainly improved a lot in the past few weeks. I watched AJ trot her spunky grey pony across the grass between the coloured fences, Squib's eyes bright and eager as he looked around at the course. Most of the fences were straight-forward, but there were a few tests – a solid brick wall, a high plank vertical and a fence with a checkerboard fill that half of the ponies in the class had been baulking at. AJ carefully steered her pony close alongside all of them before her bell sounded, and Squib obligingly spooked at each one, eyeing the wall with particular suspicion and diving sideways when asked to pass the checkerboard.

Anders stood next to me with his arms folded, watching as AJ moved Squib up into his bounding canter and rode a starting circle.

"Squib looks a bit full of himself."

"He always is," I said with a smile. "Part of what makes him so special."

Astrid stood on the other side of her brother, chewing on a fingernail and looking around vaguely. A rider on a big black horse came cantering past right behind us, and she squeaked slightly and jumped forward. Anders put a steadying hand on her back, and I watched her relax under his touch. I wasn't sure if I was jealous because it was Anders, and as much as I refused to admit it to my mother, I had a huge crush on him, or because I wished I had a big brother of my own. *It must be nice, having someone to look out for you like that.* Then AJ and Squib cleared the first jump with plenty of room to spare, and my attention was focused back on the ring.

Squib was jumping well, still a bit quicker and stronger than was ideal, but he was learning to wait and trust AJ instead of taking everything into his own hands – well, hooves. They were all clear as they made the turn towards the wall, and Squib looked at it suspiciously, seeming momentarily startled that he would be expected to jump something so solid. AJ clicked her tongue to encourage him, and he quickly rose to the challenge, launching himself over and clearing it by almost a foot. Given that this was already a metre-ten class, it was an impressive effort, and I grinned as I heard various other spectators exclaim over his scope. Riders behind us pulled up their horses and stopped to watch, and I felt a surge of pride at how well AJ was doing. She was a hard worker and had a good basic foundation, so getting her up to scratch had been pretty straightforward so far. The things she didn't know, like how to school lateral movements, or teach Squib to jump from the base instead of half a stride out, were things she'd picked up quickly, and her improvement was coming on in literal leaps and bounds.

I watched her steady up for the double, and Squib jumped cleanly through, then turned back to the planks. He strained at the bridle, pulling hard, and I could see the concentration on AJ's face as she tried to make him sit on his hocks and wait for the distance. Two strides out, I could see that it wasn't going to happen. He was coming on a long, forward stride and if she left him alone, he'd make it over cleanly. But AJ kept fighting him, and Squib threw his head up and propped, losing some of his momentum.

"Put your leg on," I hissed under my breath and she did, but it was too little, too late. Squib came in deep, and had to really push up from his hindquarters to jump the fence. He had the power, but he didn't have a fast enough reaction time in front, and his shoulders came up late. One front foot hit the plank, and it tumbled straight off the flat cups and hit the ground.

I swore, and I saw AJ shaking her head in disappointment as she continued on, muttering an apology to Squib as she turned him towards the checkerboard fence. This time she let Squib have his way, riding him forward and letting him jump off his preferred long stride. He had all the scope in the world to clear it, and he did, kicking up his hind legs so far in triumph at getting his own way that AJ looked for a moment as though she was going to tip off over his head. But she regained her seat and balanced him nicely for the last couple of fences on the course.

Scattered applause accompanied AJ out of the ring, and she patted Squib's neck enthusiastically as he jogged back over to us, looking decidedly pleased with himself.

"That was good!" I told her, and she pulled a face. "Just should've left him alone going into the planks."

"He felt like he was getting too strong and was going to jump it too flat," she told me, bringing Squib to a halt next to us and rubbing his neck. "So I took a pull and he dropped the contact. I was lucky he didn't refuse!"

"He wouldn't dream of it," I laughed. "Let you spoil his fun? No way."

Anders was standing next to Squib now, patting his sweaty neck, then clapping his sister on her leg. "You did awesome, Poss. I had no idea the Squirrel could jump so high!"

"Squib can jump way higher than that," I told him. "AJ just has to learn to keep up with him!"

AJ laughed, then turned Squib away. "I'd better walk him out, let him cool down. Come on superstar, let's move."

She rode off, and Anders turned back to me. "What happens now?"

"She got four faults, so she can't do the jump off," I explained. "So she'll cool him down and wash the sweat off him and then…"

Anders laughed, cutting me off. "I meant for you. Are you competing today?"

"Oh. Yeah. On my young one. He's in the same class, but he's way down the order so he won't be on for at least half an hour. I should get back though, see if Mum's got him tacked up yet."

Anders fell into stride next to me as we walked back to our yards, Astrid trailing behind. "Your mum's really into this horse show thing, huh?"

"Yeah. She rode as a kid, but she couldn't really afford to compete much, so she's living vicariously through me." It came out sounding a bit harsher than I meant it, and I quickly clarified. "I mean, it's great. I can't imagine what we'd have to talk about if we didn't have the ponies."

"Is that why you have so many?"

"That, and because Mum's a hoarder and keeps buying them," I told him, and he laughed.

We walked past the Maxwells' big silver truck and I saw Hayley's head swivel around, watching Anders with almost predatory interest. I quickened my pace and kept talking, hoping he wouldn't notice her. I was well aware that I couldn't compete with Hayley's glossy blonde curls, full lips and perfect body, which looked especially good in the skin-tight designer breeches that she was wearing.

I prattled on, trying to keep Anders's attention before he noticed her. "But I've only got five at the moment, because we sold Fossick, and Lucas and Robin have both gone lame. And Molly's being sold, so really I only have two." I thought for a moment. "I honestly can't remember the last time I only had two ponies to ride. I don't know what I'm going to do with myself."

"AJ told me about Molly. Sorry to hear that."

"Thanks," I said, surprised that they'd been talking about me. *What else has AJ said?* I wondered as we reached our yards to find Mum bridling Forbes.

"There you are Katy. Hello again Anders, nice to see you. Have you come to watch?"

"Thought we might as well." He glanced behind him then, as if to satisfy himself that Astrid was still tagging along. She'd stopped in front of Puppet's yard and was tentatively reaching a hand up to pat him.

"Careful, he bites," I warned her, and she snatched her hand back nervously. I pointed to Molly, standing across the aisle and looking more beautiful than a pony had any right to. "You can pat Molly though. She wouldn't hurt a fly."

Molly wandered to the front of her yard and poked her nose

over, and Astrid moved closer to her, still looking uneasy.

"I didn't mean to scare her," I told Anders, who shrugged.

"Don't worry about it. She spooks easy sometimes."

Astrid shot him a dirty look over her shoulder, and I smiled at her. "Sounds like you'll get on well with Molly then. She's always freaking out at little things like plastic bags, or leaves, or even her own shadow. I had twenty dollars in my pocket once when I went for a ride, and it fell out and started blowing away. I tried to go after it, but Molly flat out refused to go anywhere near it and before I could talk her round, it was long gone." I shook my head at the pony, who was snuffling at Astrid's hair. "Talk about throwing your money away."

"Stop chatting and get dressed, would you?" Mum said as she buckled Forbes's noseband. "You'll be on soon and you haven't even warmed him up."

"Keep your hair on," I told her, then glanced at Anders. "I'll be right back."

I'd only taken a couple of steps towards our truck before Hayley came striding into the yards, her eyes glancing off me and immediately fixing on AJ's brother.

"Hi Katy," she said with a beaming smile as she approached. At least she didn't ignore me entirely, although she probably wanted to.

"Hey." I stopped in front of her, forcing her to stop as well.

But she was still staring over my shoulder, and I knew there was no holding her back from what she wanted, so I turned and introduced them.

"Hayley, this is AJ's brother Anders, and her sister Astrid." I motioned at her. "This is Hayley."

"Hi," Hayley said, flicking her hair over her shoulder and holding out a hand to Anders to shake, her bright pink nail polish standing out against her tanned skin. He shook her hand and gave her one of his gorgeous smiles, that dimple appearing in his left cheek, and jealousy roiled around inside me.

"Katy," Mum said in her warning voice, and I rolled my eyes.

"I'm going, I'm going."

I met AJ on the way out, and scratched Squib's neck as we passed each other. "Watch out for your brother," I warned her. "Hayley's on the prowl, and she's got Anders in her sights."

"Sounds like Anders is the one who should be watching out," she replied bitterly as I headed into the truck to change.

Forbes jumped a tidy double clear, but I didn't push him in the jump off since he was still pretty green at the height. I felt a bit bad about showing up AJ's efforts in front of her family, but she was the first one to congratulate me when Forbes and I came out of the ring. We were surrounded by people, Mum and AJ on one side of my pony, and Astrid and Anders on the other, all patting Forbes and saying how well he'd gone. Mum, of course, had a couple of comments to make about how I'd ridden out of the second last turn, and that I'd been lucky going through the double the first time, but I tuned her out as much as possible.

It was when I looked over her head in an attempt to refocus my attention away from her criticism that I saw Susannah. She was standing on the other side of the ring, watching me. I'd noticed her there when I'd ridden in for the class, but I'd pushed her presence out of my mind and focused on getting Forbes around the course. She saw me watching her now, and met my eyes defiantly for a moment before turning away. Even across the distance between us, I knew what that look meant. She was determined to take Molly away from me, and she wanted me to be fully aware that she had the means to do it.

I cut off Mum's nagging and spurred Forbes forward abruptly, making him jump and Astrid scurry backwards.

"He needs walking off. Meet you back at the yards in ten."

And I turned him around and rode away from Susannah and her arrogant stare.

"We're going to get icecream. You coming?"

I looked up at AJ from where I was crouched next to Forbes, unscrewing the studs from his shoes.

"I'm not a big icecream eater," I told her, giving the spanner one last twist before dropping the stud into the box at my feet.

My bad mood still hadn't quite evaporated, as much as I wished it would. I was trying to put Susannah out of my mind, but every time I looked at Molly it made me feel sick to my stomach. To make matters worse, Steph had stopped me while I was cooling Forbes out and told me that Susannah was going to ride Molly in the Pony Grand Prix tomorrow morning, and the very thought of it was giving me heart palpitations.

"You sure?" AJ pressed. "Anders is buying."

Well, in that case... "Go on then," I replied. "Just give me a sec to get these studs done."

"Okay."

AJ went to speak to Squib again as I moved to Forbes's back legs. From the corner of my eye, I noticed someone coming into his yard. I lifted my pony's back leg and rested it on my knee, wondering idly whether the hoof black would mark my white breeches. Mum would have kittens if it did, but I couldn't be bothered getting changed and I wasn't going to leave Forbes standing around studded up for no reason.

Anders stopped next to me, his orange sneakers contrasting with my black leather tall boots.

"Taking his sprigs out?"

"Studs," I corrected his terminology. "This is show jumping, not rugby."

"Same deal though, right?" he asked as I set the spanner around the rim of the stud. "For extra traction."

"That's the idea."

I pushed down on the spanner handle to loosen the tight stud. I'd been putting studs in and out of my pony's shoes for years and could practically do it blindfolded, but of course when Anders was standing there watching me, my hand slipped. I lost my grip on the spanner and it tumbled into the shavings at our feet, and I grazed my wrist on the sharp stud. It was a new one, and still had a little nub on the end that hadn't worn away fully yet.

"Damn." I glanced at the trickle of blood running down the inside of my wrist. "That was awkward."

Anders reached down and picked up the spanner, then handed it back to me. "Need any help?"

"No, I'm good."

I reset the spanner and gripped tight this time as I loosened the stud. It resisted for a moment, and I mentally cursed my mother for having tightened them so much, but then it gave, and I was able to unscrew it without any further fuss. Hitching

Forbes's leg higher against my thigh, I unscrewed the inside one, then let his hoof down with a sigh of relief.

"Is your arm okay?"

"It's fine."

It was just a scrape, and hardly bleeding at all. It also stung like hell, but I wasn't going to admit that to him. I ran my hand across Forbes's rump as I went around to the other side of him and lifted his hind leg. Anders followed me, putting himself right into the line of fire as Forbes kicked out a couple of times, and I had to grab his leg tight to make sure Anders avoided injury.

"Woah!" He moved fast when he was startled.

"Careful," I grinned before setting to work on the studs. "He's a bit touchy with his back legs still. I think someone tried to rope him when he was a youngster, or hobbled him or something. You couldn't touch his legs at all when we got him. Or his head." I thought for a moment longer as I dropped one stud into the box. "Or lead him anywhere without him trying to run over top of you or slam you against the wall."

"He sounds crazy."

"Just misunderstood." I removed the last stud with – thankfully – no more issues, and replaced it in the stud kit with the spanner, then snapped the box shut. "Now, did someone say icecream?"

I didn't really want an icecream – I hadn't been kidding when I'd told AJ that I didn't really like the stuff – but Anders insisted on buying me one. Or, more accurately, he bought me one before I realised what he was doing, and it would've been super rude of me to say no, so I smiled and licked vaguely at it, just doing enough to keep it from running over my hands as it melted in the afternoon sun.

We sat in the grandstand and watched the Seven Year Old class, which had seemed like a good idea until Hayley found us and started drooling over Anders again. I was in the midst of rolling my eyes at AJ and wondering what excuse I could use to escape when Hayley leaned past Anders and looked at me.

"When are you going to come and try Misty?"

I smiled at her, my irritation forgotten. "Whenever you like."

She looked at her watch. "How about now?"

"Sounds good," I said as my phone buzzed in my pocket. It was Mum, and I debated ignoring her, but thought I'd better take it. "What's up?"

"I just got hold of the vet and he can come and see Robin this afternoon, so I'm packing up the truck and I need you to come back and load the ponies."

"Oh." I wondered whether to tell her about Misty, but I wanted to surprise her. She felt almost as bad as I did about my sudden lack of Grand Prix ponies, and I knew she'd be thrilled if I could take over the ride on such a good pony. "Okay, we'll be there soon."

I hung up, and turned back to Hayley. "Rain check? We've got to get home and get the vet to see Robin. But we'll be back in the morning."

"Are you riding Molly in the Grand Prix?" she asked and I reluctantly shook my head.

"Susannah is."

Hayley looked as horrified as I felt at the prospect. "On your pony? Ugh! That is *so* unfair."

"She's not really my pony," I muttered, but Hayley waved a hand dismissively.

"She might as well be, you're the only one who's ever been able to ride her. Susannah's dreaming if she thinks she'll get her around the PGP tomorrow. Oh well, maybe Molly'll throw her into the wall and shatter a few bones. Prove a point."

"Fingers crossed." I stood up, and AJ followed suit. "We'd better go."

Hayley looked as though she'd just realised what that meant. "You're *all* leaving?"

We all looked at Anders, who looked a bit like a possum in headlights under our stares. "Uh, yeah. We'd better get home, eh Chook?" he asked Astrid, who shrugged. "I'll take that as a yes," he grinned, then winked at me as he stood up.

"Come by tomorrow morning then and take Misty around the Grand Prix," Hayley told me as we made our way down the stairs. "Because over my dead body is Tess is riding him again. One more round with her in the tack and Misty'll go on strike, and I wouldn't blame him either!"

6

GOODBYES SUCK

We were late back to the show grounds the next morning, and found Susannah's mother waiting at our yards, tapping her watch pointedly as we drove in.

"I was starting to think that you weren't going to show up. I hope you've got Molly on board and she's ready to go," Naomi Andrews snapped as I jumped down from the cab and guided Mum into our spot.

I kept my back turned towards her, but she stood right behind me, practically breathing down my neck while Mum parked.

"Susie's first to go on Buckingham and ninth on Skip, then she'll be ready to ride Molly at the end of the class," Naomi told me as I hit the button to lower the hydraulic ramp.

Rub it in, why don't you? I thought to myself. Why Susannah needed three Grand Prix ponies was a mystery to me – I'd found it hard enough work with two. Forbes was nearest to the ramp and the first to come into view, and Naomi craned her neck up at him.

"There she is," Naomi said. "Bring her off and I'll get her saddled. Steph said her tack comes with her, so…"

I cut her off. "That's Forbes. Molly's further back." I let the ramp settle onto the dewy grass and went up to unload my ponies, internally fuming. The ponies' heads were hidden behind the grills, but Molly was a bright bay, and Forbes's coat was dark brown. It wasn't rocket science to tell the difference between them – even Anders had managed it yesterday and he knew nothing at all about horses. I was still mad about it as I handed Forbes off to Mum, and watched AJ go in for Squib.

I should've told Naomi to stand back. I knew that Squib liked to come off the truck with a hiss and a roar, usually jumping off from at least halfway down the ramp, but I was still angry. Besides, it wasn't my fault that Naomi thought standing right in the middle at the bottom of the ramp was a good idea. Anyone with a trace of horse sense would know that was a stupid place to stand, especially around ponies you don't know, but there's never been any telling the Andrews family anything. So AJ clipped on Squib's lead rope, and opened the divider, and Squib, true to form, took two steps forward, squealed, and jumped onto the ramp, tearing the rope out of AJ's hand. He stood goggle-eyed for a moment with all four legs planted, then launched himself off the ramp. It was Naomi's own fault that she was in the way, and she only made it worse when she shrieked and stepped backwards, instead of sideways, which would've moved her out of Squib's trajectory. But she didn't, and nearly five hundred kilograms of pony slammed into her, knocking her flat on her back.

Squib, for his part, seemed apologetic. Instead of prancing off to meet his neighbours, like he'd done the last time I'd failed to catch him on landing, he stood stock still and stared at Naomi's sprawled figure. I grabbed up his trailing lead rope as AJ came apologising down the ramp, so I left her and Mum to fuss over Naomi, taking Squib into his yard and shutting him away.

"Good job," I whispered to the pony as I unclipped his lead. "At least someone's on my side."

Naomi was back on her feet and none the worse for wear, other than a bit of mud on her impractical cream-coloured jacket. AJ was still apologising profusely as I headed past them and back up the ramp to get the next pony off, but I slowed when I realised that it was Molly.

She stood in the truck with her ears pricked, her head turned as far as it could go towards the commotion outside. I slowed my pace as I approached her, then glanced over my shoulder. They were still distracted, and I had a moment left alone with my favourite girl. I put a hand on Molly's glossy back, running my palm gently along from her withers to her loins, feeling the warm softness of her coat, the strength of her well-conditioned muscles. She shifted restlessly, ready to get out of the close quarters of the truck, and I heard Mum's voice from outside.

"Come on Katy, we're waiting for you."

I pulled back the lever that fixed the divider in place, and swung it back against the wall, then hooked it back with a bungee cord. Most of the dividers stayed back on their own, but this one had a loose pin and couldn't be relied on not to swing back and hit me in the shoulder as I tried to lead my pony out. Molly waited restlessly as I fiddled with it, until there was no more opportunity to delay. I unclipped her halter from the tie attached to the truck wall, and snapped a lead rope on in its place.

"C'mon then," I said sadly, and Molly followed me trustingly towards her fate.

Shortly afterwards, I stood outside the Maxwells' truck, looking in vain for any sign of life. Their ramp was up and their gear all stowed tidily nearby. I'd passed Misty and their other horses in their yards on my way here, still rugged and bandaged, and I was starting to have a bad feeling that Hayley had forgotten her promise to let me ride Misty in the Grand Prix today. After seeing Molly get tacked up and led away for Susannah to ride, I wanted nothing more than to go out there and kick her butt in the ring, to prove that she wasn't the only one who could get on someone else's pony and ride it successfully. I climbed the steps and rapped on the side door of Hayley's truck. There was no answer, and I knocked louder.

"Can I help you?"

I turned around to see Carmen Maxwell standing behind me with an armful of empty feed buckets, wearing jeans that were a little too tight to be appropriate on someone's mother and a well-worn pair of Ariat country boots.

"I'm looking for Hayley," I explained, jumping off the steps guiltily. The way she was looking at me made me feel like I'd been trying to break in and rob them or something.

"She's sleeping." Carmen strode towards me, her expression softening as she came closer. "Woke up with a killer headache, so she's trying to sleep it off."

I gritted my teeth, not remotely sympathetic. I knew Hayley well enough to know that she would've been out partying all night and any headache she'd woken up with was self-inflicted. I smiled at Carmen as sincerely as I could, wishing I had an ounce of the charm that people like Anders seemed to possess in spades.

"It's just that she said I could ride Misty this morning, so I came by to see if he's ready." Carmen's frown returned, and I quickly clarified my comment. "I mean, I'm happy to get him ready, I'm not expecting him tacked up or anything, but I don't know where his tack…" My voice trailed off at the look on Carmen's face, which was darkening with each word.

"I don't know what Hayley told you, but Misty is Tess's pony, and if anyone is going to ride him in the Grand Prix, it'll be her."

"Oh." I felt my skin redden, and my palms sweated anxiously. "I thought, I mean, I didn't know she was going to ride him in it."

"Well, she's won't be. Not quite up to it yet," Carmen admitted. "But Hayley doesn't get to decide who rides him and who doesn't. He's not a toy to be handed around to anyone who wants to have a go. Tess just needs time to get used to him."

"Okay." I stepped backwards and sideways, my face hot as she continued to glare at me. "I understand."

"Sorry if that disappoints you, but he's not your pony," Carmen told me sharply, as if there was any doubt left in my mind. "So you'll have to ride your own."

I would if I could, I thought angrily as I nodded and walked off, going the long way back to our truck so I wouldn't have to pass the warm-up rings and risk seeing Susannah. When I got back to our yards Mum was AWOL, but AJ was still there, diligently filling water buckets and stuffing haynets.

"Need some help?" I asked, feeling guilty that we'd left her with all the work.

"I'm almost done. Hey I meant to ask," she said, slinging Squib's haynet over the railing and struggling to tie it up while he tore mouthfuls out as though he hadn't eaten in years. "What'd the vet say about Robin?"

I groaned. "Nothing good. He isn't completely sure, but he thinks it might be navicular." I waited for AJ's horrified expression, but she just looked confused.

"What's that?"

"Navicular syndrome." She continued looking blank, so I had to call on my minimal knowledge of what it actually was, other than Something Really Bad. "Um, it's when the navicular bone starts degenerating, I think. It's a bone in the hoof," I clarified, knowing at least that much for sure. "Mostly, it's incurable. Treatable in some cases, and some horses can return to soundness after a diagnosis, but in severe cases it causes permanent lameness. Long story short, if it's navicular then his career is probably over, and it's goodbye to the pay cheque he was supposed to bring in. Not that that's the most important thing, of course, but I was kind of hoping he'd turn into this superstar show hunter pony and I could sell him for heaps and put it into the Molly fund."

AJ's expression had shifted from confusion to deep concern as I'd been talking, but my last comment had her lifting an eyebrow at me curiously. "What's the Molly fund?"

"Oh, you know. The hypothetical stash of money that would

pay for Molly so she didn't have to be sold. The one that would let me keep her." The dream was over, so I might as well talk about it. "I had this crazy idea that if we sold Robin and Forbes for decent enough money, we might be able to bargain Steph down on the asking price for Molly, so she could stay with me. But that's all gone down the toilet now that Robin's basically worthless."

"You could still sell Forbes," AJ said thoughtfully. "How much d'you reckon he'd go for?"

I shrugged. "He's still green, and a bit quirky. Not quite normal. Maybe eight grand on a good day?"

"That's not too bad," AJ said thoughtfully. "You got a bit of money from Fossick's sale too, right?"

"Not really. Mum sold her for four and a half, which *if*, and it's a pretty big if, I could get eight for Forbes, would only leave me eighteen grand short. No problem at all," I muttered sarcastically, and AJ's face fell.

"Man, I'm sorry." AJ ducked under the yard railings and abruptly wrapped her arms around me and gave me a firm hug. It felt a bit awkward, but I appreciated the gesture.

"Me too."

"So does the vet know what caused Robin's navuncular?"

"Navicular," I corrected her, grinning despite my depressed mood. "Not sure, but he said the shoeing job that Don has been doing hasn't done him any favours. Reckons his toes are left too long and it's affecting his break-over. That's the way his foot hits the ground," I explained. "Horses should land heel first and then roll across the sole and lift the toe last. Like we do. But if a horse's toes are too long, then it's a bit like us trying to walk in clown shoes. It affects the tendons in the legs as well as the internal structures of the hoof. I've been *telling* Mum for months that I don't think Don does a very good job, but she kept saying that he's been our farrier for years. I think she felt loyal to him because he would always come, even when we couldn't pay him right away. But the vet gave us the name of a new guy, so we're getting him out on Tuesday to do Robin and look at all the ponies. I can get him to check Squib too, if you want."

"Sure, if you think it's a good idea," AJ agreed as I leaned over the railing and examined what I could see of Squib's hooves. "He doesn't have shoes though."

"Yeah, I noticed. How come?"

AJ shrugged. "The people we bought him from said he doesn't need them. He's never been lame, and his hooves are hard as rock. Farriers always comment on it."

"Fair enough," I replied. "He might need them one day though, when you want to put studs in for the bigger jumps. Give him more grip off the ground, and on the turns."

AJ looked indecisive. "I guess we'll cross that bridge when we come to it. He doesn't seem to be having any problems so far, so for now we'll just carry on as we are."

Our classes weren't until later in the day, but AJ and I got sick of standing around, so we saddled Squib and Puppet and took them for a ride, leaving Forbes to devour his haynet and chat with the big chestnut horse in the yard next to him. Squib was his usual exuberant self, walking as though his legs were on springs, spooking at every little thing that moved and winding

Puppet up so much that by the time we'd been out for twenty minutes, our legs were sore and bruised from being cannoned into by one another's ponies.

"Let's never ride these two together again," I grumbled as a kid rode past on a bike and Puppet leapt into Squib, slamming my ankle into AJ's stirrup iron for what felt like the thousandth time. Maybe bringing Puppet along for the outing hadn't been such a brainwave after all.

"They're as pathetic as each other," AJ agreed. "Oh for goodness' sake Squib, it's a piece of cardboard, it's not going to eat you."

Squib didn't believe her, stopping dead and snorting loudly, his neck arched like a stallion as he pretended that the crushed paper cup on the ground just ahead of us was the most terrifying thing a pony had ever faced.

"I don't see how he can jump the scariest jumps without batting an eyelid, but he can't handle a bit of rubbish on the ground," AJ grumbled as Squib blithely ignored her attempts to kick him on past it.

"He's deeply offended by litter," I grinned, trying to get Puppet to lead the way forward, but he was easily influenced and had decided that if Squib said it was too dangerous to proceed, he was probably right. "He thinks we should be tidier Kiwis."

AJ snorted. "Any excuse to be an idiot, more like," she grumbled. "Come on Squibward or I'll take you home right now and you won't get to do any jumping today."

Squib took one step forward, then spun on his hocks and bounded across the grass with his head in the air, fleeing the terrifying paper cup. I managed to keep Puppet from following him, but not without having to sit a few frantic pigroots and a half-decent attempt at a rear.

"Honestly Puppet, I thought you were a good boy," I muttered. "You've made your bed now. I don't care if we're here for hours, you are going up to that bit of stupid trash and sniffing it if it's the last thing you ever do." I sat down in the saddle and shortened my reins, keeping my contact firm but gentle, and closed my legs around his sides. "Just take it one step at a time."

Puppet threw his head from side to side, then tried to turn around and look for Squib. I resisted the temptation myself, confident that AJ would've got her pony back under control by now, and focused on getting Puppet to walk forward. Slowly, one hoof at a time, Puppet crept reluctantly towards the paper cup. He was still about three metres away from it when I realised that someone was riding towards us, and I glanced up, about to apologise for blocking the path, until I realised who it was.

Molly pricked her ears and fluttered her nostrils at Puppet in greeting, and I swallowed hard.

"Having trouble?" Susannah asked mockingly.

"He's just being an egg," I muttered. "He's only four."

"He's cute," she said, and I shot her a suspicious look, wondering if she was making fun of Puppet. He resembled nothing more than a black giraffe, a long weedy neck, legs that ended in pigeon-toed feet, and a roach back. Even his tiny white star didn't do his face any favours, sitting higher than was attractive and emphasising the bump between his eyes. Nobody in their right mind would describe him as cute.

Under the pressure of Susannah's gaze as she waited to get through the narrow space, I nudged Puppet forward a bit too forcefully. He promptly had a meltdown, running backwards and almost crashing into some people who were ignorant enough to have tried to walk behind him, nearly crushing them into the fence. They grumbled at me, as if it wasn't their own fault for putting themselves into the firing line, and Susannah shifted restlessly in Molly's saddle.

"Why doesn't Molly give him a lead past?" she offered, sounding bored.

I shook my head. "He'll go past. I want him to walk up to it. I'm not letting him think he can pack tantrums like this." I took a breath, tried to calm my own energy. "If it takes an hour then it takes an hour, but once he learns that if he spooks at something this badly then he's going to have to approach and sniff it, he'll start to relax more when he sees something that bothers him."

Susannah looked at me sceptically. "Sounds counter-productive to me."

"Well, that shows how much you know," I snapped back.

"I just meant, if he's scared of something then surely making him go and sniff it would just upset him. Why not teach him that if he's scared, that you won't make him go into the danger zone, so he trusts you to keep him safe?"

The annoying part was that she partly made sense. But that wasn't how I did things, and I wasn't about to change now after my way had worked for years.

"He has to face his fears," I told her, urging Puppet on, and he moved reluctantly forward. It was only half a step, but as soon as he took it I relaxed, taking the pressure off with my legs and letting the reins sit loose on his neck, giving him a chance to relax his mind and muscles before I asked him to take another one.

Baby steps, Mum called it. *Granny steps* was how I thought of it, but either way it worked…eventually. But it took time, and I was becoming increasingly aware of the other horses and ponies that were now trying to get through the narrow gap that the paper cup happened to be in. Just as I got Puppet to take another hesitant step forward, Susannah's father walked up behind her, slapping Molly on the rump and startling the pony.

To her credit, Susannah glowered down at her father. "You scared her!"

"She's fine," he bluffed, clapping Molly's neck and making her flinch.

I scowled at him, my attention diverted from Puppet for a moment. "She hates being patted like that."

He didn't look too happy to see me. "Are you having some problems?" He walked closer. "Want me to lead him?" His hand reached forward towards Puppet's bridle, and my blood chilled at the thought of him dragging the pony forward.

"No!" I said emphatically. "He's fine. I just need to get him to relax a bit, and then…" I closed my leg again and Puppet lifted a foreleg, then lowered it again in the same place, still snorting suspiciously at the terrifying paper cup.

Derrick turned his head and saw the offensive object lying in the grass. "Is that what's bothering him?" he asked, then walked over and picked it up.

Puppet snorted loudly, eyes boggling, then watched

suspiciously as Derrick held it out to Molly, who sniffed it without interest. He turned towards Puppet, holding the flattened cup out in front of him, and Puppet watched nervously as Derrick strode up and shoved it in his face. For a moment, I felt Pup's muscles tense, tightening like a bow string under pressure, ready at any second to release into a headlong flight. Then he abruptly decided not to be scared anymore and relaxed, sniffing calmly at the paper cup and then turning his head away with a bored expression. I could've killed him.

"He's fine now," Derrick said, as though I couldn't tell. "Come on, Susie. Steph said she'd meet us at the O'Reilly's truck."

I felt the hackles on the back of my neck rise as he talked about me as though I wasn't right there in front of them. Susannah looked embarrassed as she rode Molly past, and it was then that I noticed the green ribbon around Molly's muscular neck. Fourth place in the Grand Prix. And it had been a big class today – I'd looked at the entries online last night. Nineteen competitors, and some of them were form combinations. As much as I hated to admit it, Molly was clearly going well for her. Which meant that any lingering hopes that I'd harboured of Susannah changing her mind and not wanting Molly were well and truly dashed, and my pony was as good as gone.

I didn't get much of a chance to say goodbye. After returning Molly to her yard, Susannah had gone off to look after her other two ponies, both of which had also jumped double clears in the Grand Prix to finish second and fifth, but she was back less than an hour later. I was saddling Forbes for the metre-ten when she turned up with her parents and Steph Marshall in tow, and I knew what was coming.

"She's sound as a bell," Steph was saying as they strode down the aisle. Susannah had a leather headcollar over her shoulder and was idly thwacking the end of the cotton lead rope against her leg as she walked. "Hardly been lame a day in her life, this pony."

That's not true, I wanted to say, but Derrick spoke up before I could.

"I thought Susie said she'd gone lame last season."

Steph hesitated for a moment, then either remembered or was forced to admit it. "She had a mild ligament tear last season, that's true. But she was rehabbed very slowly and carefully, and has perfectly clean scans. And other than that – sound as a bell."

Still not true. There was also the time she'd developed a stone bruise and acted as though her leg was falling off, limping around dramatically for days despite the bute that Mum had been dosing her up on. And the time that she'd had a wither abscess that had forced me to ride her bareback for weeks on end. And the day that Don had done a worse job of shoeing than usual and pricked her with a nail. It'd been weeks before she'd recovered fully from that one, though I suspected that it was mostly emotional trauma. Molly's threshold for pain had always been low.

Steph stopped in front of Molly's yard and patted her neck firmly, making Molly twitch. *Steph doesn't even know her,* I thought sadly as I listened to her prattle on. *She has no idea what makes Molly tick.* I could've contradicted her comments countless times if anyone had thought to ask me – but nobody did. As Molly sidled away from Steph and went to stand on the other side of her yard, I realised something that I hadn't quite put together before.

Steph doesn't even like her.

I'd long suspected that Molly didn't like Steph much, but for some reason it hadn't occurred to me that Steph didn't like Molly either. I wondered why. She was such a good rider, and she could get on and ride anything. I'd seen her do it, jump clear rounds on horses whose owners couldn't get them through the start flags, but for some reason, she'd never clicked with Molly.

But I had. And unfortunately, based on how well she'd been going for her, Susannah had too.

I had to turn away then, leaning against Forbes's shoulder as they stood across the aisle and discussed the terms of Molly's sale. Derrick was doing his best to talk Steph into giving them a week's trial before they committed to the purchase, but Steph was of the opinion that they already knew they wanted her, so what was holding them back?

"We'll want to get her thoroughly vetted," Derrick said firmly. "No surprises."

"I told you, she's completely sound," Steph argued. "Look, write me a cheque and I'll give you a week to get her vetted. If she fails, which she won't, then I'll tear up the cheque and you can send her back. If I don't hear from you, I bank the cheque next Monday."

I admired the steel in her voice, even as I hated the words she was saying. Derrick Andrews was used to intimidating people, but although Steph was only a fraction over five feet tall, she knew how to stand up for herself. I turned slowly around and watched as Derrick shook her hand, then nodded to his daughter. Susannah stepped into Molly's yard and removed my halter, then buckled her own one on in its place. And I just stood there, unable to do anything other than watch as she led Molly out of my life.

7
MEMORY LANE

It had been a hot day in the middle of summer when we'd first gone up to Gisborne to see Molly. I'd been a shy twelve-year-old, looking around me in awe as Mum drove up the tree-lined driveway of Westbrook stud, and parked her shabby little Mazda in front of the house. Kat Marshall had come out to greet us with her arms wide open and an even wider smile on her face.

"Deb! You made it!"

Mum had known Kat since before I was born, when she'd taken a job as a research clerk at a small law firm. Kat's husband Ben owned the company, and they'd hit it off when Kat came in one day dressed in riding clothes. Mum had been away from horses for a few years at that stage, but meeting Kat and her young daughters had inspired her to get back into the equestrian world – one she hadn't left since.

I had climbed out of the car and stood there self-consciously as Mum and Kat embraced each other. I'd only met Kat a handful of times before at shows, and her daughters Samantha and Stephanie had appeared polished and professional - leagues above where I was at with my small ponies, pottering around the show hunter rings.

Kat had greeted me with a warm smile but hadn't tried to hug me, perhaps sensing that I wouldn't welcome it from someone I still considered a stranger. I've never been very outgoing with people I don't know well, and Kat was one of those overly friendly people that always made me feel even shyer around them. We'd followed her into the house and I'd sat at the kitchen table nibbling half-heartedly on a biscuit while they drank tea and gossiped.

Sam had saved me from total boredom when she came into the room. She was the image of her mother with the same thick blonde hair and vivid blue eyes that crinkled at the corners when she smiled, and she overflowed with confidence and enthusiasm. Unlike Steph, who always had an air of arrogance around her, Sam was friendly and down-to-earth. She was also one of the best riders I'd ever seen in the saddle, and was considered, even then, to be a rising star of the New Zealand equestrian world.

"Hi Katy," she'd said. "How's your little chestnut pony? Still trying to launch you into outer space?"

I'd smiled back, surprised that she'd remembered. She'd seen me riding Kiwi at a show a few weeks earlier. He'd been giving me a bit of trouble, because that was Kiwi's way, and had been trying to buck me off every time I asked for a flying change. I'd come out of the ring deeply frustrated, and Sam had taken me aside and given me a quick lesson in asking for smoother changes. It wasn't anything different from what Mum had been trying to tell me for weeks, but somehow it had sunk in better when it came from Sam, and I'd gone back into the ring and won my next two rounds.

"He's much better," I'd told her, and she'd smiled even wider as she poured herself a glass of water from the tap.

"That's great. You've come to ride Molly today, I hear?" I'd nodded, swallowing nervously. It had still seemed incredible to me that someone was offering me a quality full-size show jumping pony to ride, and I wouldn't quite believe it until it happened. "She's down at the barn now if you want to come see her. Save you sitting around here getting bored."

So I'd followed Sam down to their large barn, past paddocks full of some of the most beautiful ponies I'd ever seen. I'd fallen in love with Molly as soon as I'd seen her, and had spent at least half an hour grooming her while Sam tacked up one of her horses and took him out to the arena to ride. I'd gone out to watch her, and that's where Mum and Deb had found us when they'd finally finished catching up.

"That's a nice little horse," Mum had said, watching Sam canter the small black Thoroughbred around the arena.

"Sam really rates that one," Kat had replied. "Says he'll go all the way. I'm not sure yet, but he's certainly got a lot of scope and just won his first two-star. Not bad for a racetrack reject!"

We'd stayed to watch Sam finish up her ride, and three years later, when she took the same horse to the UK and ran him double clear around Badminton to finish in eighth place, everyone had sat up and noticed the little black gelding that she called Kingdom Come.

I still remember the first time I sat in Molly's saddle. She'd been wired, stepping nervously under me and twitching her ears back and forth constantly as we rode. Sam had walked out into the middle of the arena with me and chatted calmly as we circled around her.

"She hasn't had much work lately, so you're not seeing her at her best," Sam admitted. "But it won't take long for her to muscle up again." She'd grinned up at me, squinting through the midday sun. "How's she feel?"

"Big," I'd replied honestly, and Sam had laughed.

"Bit bigger than your wee ponies," she'd agreed. "She's got a life cert at fourteen-two though, so she's definitely a pony, just one at the bigger end of the scale. Shorten your reins a bit, and think about trotting."

That day, that ride, had changed my life. I'd never ridden a pony like Molly before. She was so sensitive, so attuned to my movements and thoughts that, as Sam had hinted, all I had to do was think about trotting, and we were doing it. If I thought about trotting slowly, Molly slowed, and when I pictured us walking on a loose rein, Molly agreed to it. Riding her was like a mind-meld, a perfect symbiosis of horse and human, working together in partnership. It hadn't been entirely perfect, of course. Molly was wired and out of shape, and I was a skinny kid with only a vague idea of what I was doing, but by the end of a half hour we were cantering smooth figure eights with flying changes in the middle, and I was having the time of my life.

And when Sam had put up some jumps, Molly had flown over all of them. She'd rushed a bit at first, feeling nervous and unsettled under me, but I had just focused on staying calm and finding a good distance, and after a while her pace had slowed to match me. Sam had told me to have fun and wandered off to the gate, where Mum and Kat were watching from, and I'd taken Molly around the whole course of jumps, putting her at anything I thought she was capable of, totally unfazed by the unfamiliar bigger heights. When she was puffing and sweating, I'd brought her back to a walk and taken her over to my spectators, feeling slightly guilty about working her so hard when Sam had warned me that she was out of shape.

But they were all grinning at me, and I'd even caught Kat wiping a tear from the corner of her eye.

"That was wonderful, Katy," she'd told me. "I've never seen Molly look so happy."

And so that had been that, and Molly had come home with us, much to my incredulous disbelief. I hadn't even seen Steph that day, and I'd been worried that she would be upset about Molly leaving, but Kat had reassured me that her youngest daughter would hardly notice that she was gone.

My first Pony Club rally on Molly came up a couple of weeks later, and I'll never forget it. I used to go to Pony Club rallies a lot back then. Mum would coach and I would ride, taking a different pony every time, and often taking two ponies down and riding one before the rally started. But the truck wouldn't start that day, and once we'd finally got it up and running, we'd ended up arriving fifteen minutes late.

We'd dragged Molly off the truck and Mum had dashed off to coach, leaving me to tack up as quickly as I could on my own. Molly had sensed my anticipation and was bursting out of her skin by the time I was in the saddle, and I remember feeling a sense of foreboding as we'd made our way towards our assigned group. Molly was on her toes, looking around nervously at everyone and spooking at anything that moved, and I was starting to wonder for the first time if I'd bitten off more than I could chew. She felt bigger than ever, and I've always been small for my age. Even at twelve, my legs barely reached past the saddle flaps, and I had felt ridiculously over-horsed all of a sudden.

It hadn't helped that Donna, who was coaching me that day, had stared at me as though I'd turned up to rally on a pony with three heads. I'd been bursting with excitement at the prospect of turning up on Molly, had expected the other riders to gather round and admire her. I'd predicted that they'd ask me thousands of questions, and when they wanted to know her show name, I would proudly say *Westbrook Double Trouble*, and they'd know that she had come from a top show jumping stud, and would be able to kick their ponies' butts into next week. But nobody had asked, and by the end of the rally, I wasn't about to tell them either.

The Marshalls had warned me that Molly had always schooled well enough at home but was unpredictable at shows. Sometimes she'd jumped clear rounds with Steph, and had won classes up to 1.15m. But she was also easily wound up, had a propensity for refusals, and as I later found out, had quite the reputation in the ring for smashing jumps. She'd been going beautifully for me at home, and I had never even felt like she was going to refuse at a fence. But at that Pony Club rally, everything had changed. Molly went from smooth and rideable to wild and unmanageable. She'd reared several times, pigrooted if I asked her to move away from the other ponies, and refused point blank to go anywhere near a jump. Donna had shoved a whip into my hand and told me to make Molly behave, but I'd dropped it immediately when Molly had threatened to bolt. Eventually I had taken her away to a corner and tried to school her in circles, but even that had been almost impossible. She'd pulled hard and run through the bridle, making my arms ache. I'd come back to the group to just stand and watch, and Molly had sidled restlessly and pawed the ground.

When Mum had eventually finished teaching her group and come over to see how I was getting on, I'd been near tears. My beautiful Molly had disappeared and been replaced by a mad pony that I couldn't ride. But when Donna had turned to Mum and told her that she was crazy for putting me on such a useless pony that was never going to be any good, I'd taken her comments as a personal challenge. I knew that there was nothing wrong with Molly. It was all me, and it was my responsibility as her new rider to do my best by her, and to get her to behave.

Mum had been dubious for a while that I would learn to cope with her, but whenever Kat rang and asked how the pony was getting on, we'd both say that Molly was wonderful, amazing, perfect. We'd both fallen in love with her, and neither of us wanted to admit that things weren't working the way we'd anticipated. And we didn't want the Marshalls to think that giving her to me to ride had been a bad decision, so we'd put a brave face on and insisted that everything was just fine.

Even back then, Molly had been fussy about eating, and

Mum had shut her into the stable one night to finish her feed while we had dinner. We'd both forgotten about her, and it wasn't until I'd woken up at midnight that I'd remembered that Molly was still shut inside. I'd got up and grabbed a torch, then gone out to the stables to let her out.

Molly had been standing at the front of her stable, staring out across the yard. She'd looked so beautiful in the moonlight, and I'd gone up to her and given her a big hug. I'd been about to put her halter on when I'd discovered that she still hadn't finished her feed.

"You have to eat," I'd whispered to my pony, and scooped out a handful of the damp mixture and held it out to her.

Molly had followed me across the loosebox and snuffled at my outstretched hand, then carefully eaten the feed off my palm. I'd scooped out another handful, and another, and Molly had quietly eaten all of it. When the bucket was empty, I'd taken hold of her neck rug and led her out of the box and down to the paddock, trusting her to walk sensibly beside me, and she had. I'd let her go, but she'd stayed just inside the gate and gently nuzzled me while I leaned on the fence and talked to her. I don't know how long we were out there, but it wasn't until I was shivering from the cold and my bare feet had turned numb that I'd eventually kissed her goodnight and gone inside.

The next morning, Molly had whinnied to me when she saw me coming, and a week later we'd gone to our first show together. We'd entered into the ring at a floating trot, Mum's words echoing in my ears. *Just do your best. Ride her as well as you can, and treat her like a princess no matter what.*

I'd drawn Molly to a slightly reluctant halt in front of the judge's truck, and Donna had looked down at me disparagingly.

"This is ambitious," she'd said, looking at Molly who was sidling restlessly.

I didn't think ninety centimetres was ambitious at all, but I supposed that for all she knew, Molly had never gone near a jump in her life. I'd fixed her with my most determined stare as the other judge in the truck had asked for my pony's name, and had made sure that I was watching Donna's face as I spoke.

"Westbrook Double Trouble," I'd told her proudly, and as predicted, Donna's expression had been priceless. Her jaw dropped a couple of inches, her eyes widened, then squinted in suspicion, but the other judge was already speaking.

"So it is! I know this pony. Good luck," the nice judge had said, smiling at me as she rang the bell, and I'd sent Molly off into her smooth canter.

Molly had been amazing that day, jumping a super double clear round and winning the class. Not that Donna had been able to resist having another dig at me when she'd come out of the truck to tie the ribbon around Molly's neck. She'd looked up at me, sitting so proud in my wonderful pony's saddle, and done her best to take the shine off my success.

"Well aren't you lucky," she'd said. "To have a pony like this to ride, with all the work done for you."

As though I'd spent my life riding schoolmasters, instead of breaking in ponies and schooling them for sale. As if I hadn't spent two months last winter schooling her daughter's pony back to rideability after she'd almost destroyed his mouth by riding him in a Pelham with draw reins because she had no seat and couldn't control him when he got a bit frisky. I'd scowled down at her and tried to think of something suitably cutting to say in response, but the other judge had intervened.

"I haven't seen this this pony jump so well in years," she'd told me with a genuine smile. "You gave her a super ride. Well done."

I'd clung onto those words then, and never forgot them. Especially when I started taking Molly out at the registered shows, and had soon discovered that nobody had particularly high expectations of her. Mum and I had heard plenty of comments from the sidelines, especially in those early days.

She's going well now, but wait 'til the jumps get bigger.

Nice-looking pony, but it's got a dirty stop and it knows how to use it.

Steph said it turned dog on her.

Bit of a foul trick to lump a young kid with a pony like that.

But slowly and surely, Molly and I had proven ourselves. It hadn't happened overnight. There had been bad days, days when Molly reverted to being an uncontrollable wild child, days when I'd lost my temper with her, days when she would refuse the jumps for apparently no reason. Our first trip to Nationals, all the way down in the South Island, had been a bit of a disaster, at least as far as Molly was concerned. I'd had Lucas too by then, but it was Molly that I'd wanted to do well on, to prove her worth – and mine. We'd started well, only to have a refusal at the first fence in our jump off for the title class, knocking us right out contention.

And then there'd been the agony of the day last December when I'd found her limping in the paddock, and discovered that she'd partially torn a ligament. I'd nursed her back to health, slowly and surely, writing off the rest of that season so that I could give her every chance to return to full soundness. Starting out walking, then trotting, and finally cantering and jumping. Schooling her steadily over winter, training her up until she was so rideable, so fit and strong and balanced and willing, that I'd just known that this was going to be our best season yet.

And now she was gone, and all of my hopes and dreams gone with her.

8

FIRST FIFTEEN

"Sit up, bring your shoulders back. Balance him!"

I stood in the middle of our arena, ignoring Critter scrabbling at my ankles and asking to be picked up as I watched AJ canter Squib out of the corner towards the jump. His bounding stride covered the ground effortlessly and he sized up the jump with an eager look on his expressive face. I could see AJ's intense focus, and watched proudly as she found a perfect distance to the base of the oxer, folded forward as Squib took off, and sat up smoothly on landing, guiding him around the corner to the vertical.

"That was perfect! Stay as you are, don't let him get quick."

I could see from the ground what the adrenalin pumping through AJ's veins disguised to her, the gradual increase in speed and lengthening of Squib's stride as he approached the high vertical. I watched AJ listen to me and steady him, approving of the way that she used her weight and a firm but steady contact on the reins to bring him back to the pace she wanted. She'd improved so much in the past few weeks, it was hard to believe she was the same rider who'd been careening around at Pony Club when I met her, completely out of control. I hadn't thought much of her then, but I'd changed my mind fast when I'd realised how willing she was to learn, and improve. And how incredibly cute Squib was when he jumped.

The dark grey gelding tucked his forelegs tight against his belly as he cleared the vertical, and AJ looked left as they landed. Squib cantered into the turn on the wrong lead, and I called out to AJ to fix it. Squib hadn't quite mastered flying changes yet, so she brought him back to a trot, then asked him to canter again. He bounded forward so enthusiastically that I couldn't help laughing, and I grinned as they soared over the last two jumps on our makeshift course.

"Super. Perfect. All the high fives to Squib."

My friend was breathless and beaming as she eased her exuberant pony back to a trot, and looked at the high jumps in disbelief.

"I can't believe we just did that!"

"Believe it," I told her. "Didn't I tell you that he'd be jumping Grand Prix by the end of the season? Only a few holes higher on these stands and you'll be maxing out the pony heights."

AJ walked squib on a loose rein, her feet kicked free of the stirrups. "How big does the Pony Grand Prix get?"

"Metre-thirty-five, at three-star level. Metre-thirty at two-star, metre-twenty-five at one-star. Basically. Those are the maximum heights, anyway. They don't usually build everything to height, except in classes like Pony of the Year."

AJ shook her head. "It still seems like an impossible dream."

"Not nearly," I assured her. "Not on a jumping machine like Squib!"

AJ grinned at me, then looked over towards our yard as we

heard the crunch of tyres on gravel. "Who's that?"

"Must be the new farrier," I said, recalling that he was due today. "Coming to look at Robin. I'd better get over there."

The new farrier was just stepping out of his dusty grey ute when I walked up. He was quite old, maybe fifty or so, with flecked grey hair and matching stubble. He smiled at me as he shut the door behind him and pulled his chaps out of the back canopy.

"Morning. Rick Conrad," he introduced himself, taking my hand in his large, scuffed one and shaking it firmly. He had a competent, experienced air about him that I immediately liked, and I returned his friendly smile.

"Katy O'Reilly. Nice to meet you. Thanks for coming to see Robin."

"Not a problem. Is this the young man in question?" He was looking at Lucas, so I redirected him.

"No, that one's got a strained ligament. This is the other hospital case."

"Rough luck, having two of them out at once," he commiserated, and I just shrugged, not wanting to get into just how much bad luck I'd been having lately. "Bring him out then, let's have a look."

Rick was removing Robin's shoes a few minutes later when AJ rode back into the yard on a much cooler and calmer Squib, and I introduced them. I noticed him watching Squib walk past, and when AJ had shut him into a box near the tack room, I asked what he thought.

"Of the grey? Nice-looking pony. Well-built. Energetic type, would go all day." He grinned at me as he picked up his rasp and started shaping Robin's hoof. "Is that what you wanted to know?"

"I meant about his hooves. He's not shod." I couldn't explain why it was bothering me all of a sudden, but it was. If AJ wanted to jump Squib in the Grand Prix, she was going to have to use studs, or he'd slip right over on the grass and have a nasty accident. I'd always assumed that she would just shoe him when the time came, but she'd become increasingly cagey about it every time I brought it up, and when I'd suggested that she get Rick to shoe him on his visit today, she'd flat out refused.

"Doesn't seem to be bothering him too much," was all that Rick said. "Does he have trouble, is he feeling the ground?"

I was forced to shake my head. "No."

"He'll be right. Ponies like that have feet like rock. Ponies like this one, on the other hand," he'd continued, snapping my attention back to the pony in front of me, "are not so genetically blessed. We're dealing with some funky-shaped hooves right here, and it's not entirely down to bad shoeing, though that is part of it, unfortunately."

I'd never paid much attention to my ponies' hooves before, but then Don had never spent much time explaining things either. Just cut and rasped away the excess wall, whacked a shoe into an approximate shape, and nailed it on. Rick explained what he was doing as he worked, telling us why he was trimming the way he was, how ideally he'd take more toe off but he wanted to do it in increments so it wasn't too uncomfortable for Robin, and why he'd chosen to use rubber pads and bar shoes to relieve the heel pain in the meantime. After a while it started going over my head, but AJ had come over and was listening with rapt attention, so I did my best to stay focused, hoping Rick would influence her into seeing the sense in shoeing Squib.

By the time he'd come to fitting Robin's back shoes though, we'd run out of hoof-related explanations and had moved on to more ordinary topics, like where we went to school, and whether we knew his son Harry who, as it transpired, went to our school but was a year older. I'd winked at AJ when he'd brought it up, and given her a little nudge that she'd returned tenfold, sending me sprawling against the wall and startling Robin into kicking out, which in turn made Rick mutter something unsavoury under his breath.

"Now I know you're a real farrier," AJ told him with a grin. "I thought for a minute there you must be a fraud, since I hadn't heard you swear yet."

Rick laughed, setting down Robin's hoof and straightening his back. Trickles of sweat were running down his forehead and he wiped them off with the back of his hand.

"First thing they teach you at farrier school," he assured AJ. "How to swear like a sailor in front of impressionable young clients."

Mum turned up then and diverted his attention for a while, and I grew bored and went inside for something to drink. I was feeling hungry, but there was nothing in our pantry that looked very appealing, so in the end I settled for half an apple. I tried not to look at the photos of Molly on the wall, or the sashes she'd won that were hanging over the fireplace. I tried not to think about her at all.

"Wait!"

I ran towards the departing bus as it pulled out of the high school car park, but all I got was a face full of diesel fumes, and I used all of the most colourful language that I'd learned from farriers over the years to vent my frustration. That was the last bus, and I'd missed it. Mum was at work in Napier and she wouldn't finish until 5pm. I knew that, and I still rang her, because I was frustrated and annoyed and couldn't think of what else to do. It didn't help. She impatiently told me that I should run faster next time, and I would have to get the next bus.

"But there won't be one for ages!"

"Not my problem, Katy. Wait or walk, those are your options. I have to go." And she'd hung up before I could argue the point.

I scowled at my phone, then went to check the timetable on the bus shelter, where I discovered that the next bus wouldn't arrive for almost forty-five minutes. I swore some more, just in case it helped. Other than making me feel slightly better, it didn't, but I noticed something else that did.

It was the First XV rugby team, training on the adjacent sports field. I wasn't much of a rugby fan, but a player in the middle of the field with blonde hair and broad shoulders had caught my attention. I'd recognise Anders from a mile away, even if he wasn't wearing the Number 15 jersey, which even I knew meant was the fullback position. He was running backwards now, his eyes fixed on the rugby ball that was spiralling through the air towards him. I watched as he caught it, then dropped it onto his boot and punted it back downfield. His teammate caught it in turn and fired it straight back at Anders, which I supposed meant they were doing some kind of kicking and catching drill. But the other guy had overcooked it, and it sailed high over Anders's head and hit the ground a few metres behind him, bouncing awkwardly as only a rugby ball can do, and coming straight towards me.

I flinched, ball sports being a long way from my forte, but fortunately the ball bounced again and pivoted off to the side before dribbling to a stop. Anders jogged towards it, then noticed me and grinned, and the butterflies in my stomach erupted into chaos.

"Hey Katy."

"Hi." I aimed for nonchalance and missed, my voice coming out squeaky and desperate.

"You miss the bus?"

"Yeah." I wished I could think of something more interesting to say, but my brain was too busy noticing how tall he was, and how good he looked in his rugby uniform, and how the corners of his mouth quirked upwards when he smiled, to think of anything smart or clever.

Anders leaned down and swept the ball up off the ground in one easy motion. "There'll be one at half four."

"I know. I guess I'm stuck waiting."

He juggled the ball from hand to hand. "Guess so. Unless you want to join practice? We could use a spare tackle bag."

"Haha," I said, deadpan, and his smile grew wider until that dimple appeared. *Oh, help. How can anyone actually be so good-looking?*

"You sure? I promise to be gentle." He was still standing

there, still smiling at me, and my mouth went dry. *Was he flirting with me?* I felt my palms starting to sweat as I tried to formulate an answer, but then Anders's teammate yelled at him from downfield to come back and get on with it. He rolled his eyes at me. "Better get back to it. See ya."

"Bye."

I watched him run away from me, then pause mid-stride and fire off another long kick before jogging back into position. I looked at my watch. Ten to four. Well, I might as enjoy the scenery while I waited, so I dropped my bag onto the grass bank that surrounded the rugby field and sat down. I pulled out my Bio textbook and pretended to be studying from it while surreptitiously watching the players practice. Okay, watching Anders practice. There were a couple of other decent-looking guys on the team, but none of them held a candle to Anders Maclean. I couldn't decide whether it was bad luck that he was AJ's brother, which made him off limits to me, or good luck that he was AJ's brother, which meant that he knew who I was, and gave me the excuse to talk to him.

My stomach rumbled, and I fished out a half-eaten muesli bar and nibbled at it as I waited. The minutes ticked past, and I knew I should get up soon and walk to the bus stop so I didn't miss the next bus, but I couldn't convince my legs to move. Not until I heard a car slow to a stop behind me, and I turned to see a big black Range Rover pull up on the gravel. *Oh no. Please, no. How did he know I was here?*

My father stepped out of the car and walked towards me, his jeans and polo shirt making him look like he was trying way too hard to be trendy. He pushed his sunglasses up into his thick dark hair and I glared at him as he walked up and stopped in front of me.

"What're you doing here?" I demanded.

"I came to pick you up. Heard you missed the bus."

How in the hell did he... "Did Mum ring you?" I couldn't believe the level of betrayal, but he shook his head.

"I called her, actually. Wanted to take you out for dinner, have a catch up, but there was nobody home when I went over so I gave Deb's cell a ring, and she told me where you were."

"That's trespassing," I told him. "You can't just turn up at our place whenever you like."

Dad frowned, his expression darkening. "Come on now, Katy. Get in the car."

"No way! I'd rather walk home than go anywhere with you."

He looked exasperated. "I'm still your father," he reminded me.

"Yeah, well if you wanted to be my father you should've stuck around and acted like one," I told him ruthlessly.

"That's not fair," he argued, and I gave a short, disbelieving laugh.

"*That's* not fair? I'll tell you what's not fair. Running off to Australia and pretending we don't exist. Shirking your child support payments and making us live on rice and beans for months on end. Making me have to go to school in second-hand uniform," and my throat clenched up on those words. I *hated* wearing other people's clothes. Dad looked like he was about to say something, so I kept talking before he could interject. "And don't you dare tell me you fell in love or something gross. You were *supposed* to be in love with Mum, remember?"

Dad was looking horrified, and I realised that the entire First XV were staring at us. They'd finished practice and were heading towards the sheds to change, and I felt my face flush with embarrassment at the scene we were making.

"We definitely need to talk," Dad said. "But not here. Get in the car, and we'll go somewhere more private."

I got to my feet, stuffing my books into my bag. "I'm not going anywhere with you."

"Is everything okay?" I looked up to see Anders walking towards us, looking concerned.

Dad turned and looked at him, and more than ever, I wished that Anders was my boyfriend and was here to rescue me. Wouldn't that just be a kick in the teeth for my father?

"I'm *not* getting in the car with you," I repeated to Dad, and I watched Anders's concern turn into immediate defence.

"You heard her." He stepped closer to me, smelling of sweat and grass and body spray, and I knew I'd never been more grateful in my life to have someone standing next to me. *Is this what falling in love feels like?* I thought for a second as Anders's arm bumped against mine, making my skin prickle. "Maybe you should clear off and leave her alone."

"I'm her father," Dad told Anders firmly, and from the corner of my eye I saw him glance at me with a confused frown, probably wondering what he'd put himself into the middle of.

"I don't care if you're the King of the world, I'm not going anywhere with you," I informed my father. I looked over at the rest of Anders's team climbing into the bus, which had pulled up at the stop moments earlier. "And now you're making me miss my bus."

I grabbed my bag and tried to take a step towards it, but Dad moved in front of me, blocking my progress. I was starting to see red when Anders reached out and grabbed my hand, closing his fingers around my balled up fist. Just then, I was too angry to properly appreciate it, but I could feel my skin starting to tingle against his sweaty palm.

"I'll give Katy a ride." He was talking to Dad, not even asking me, but I was hardly going to argue. "I know where she lives."

The look on Dad's face was priceless as he immediately sized Anders up, and again I wished that he really was my boyfriend, and that he'd always be there to stand up against my dad. He could probably take him, too. Dad was reasonably fit and trim, with none of the extra pounds that other people's fathers carried around, but Anders was younger and stronger. The muscles in his arms were tensed as he stared Dad down, and I shifted my weight closer to him, trying to add to the illusion.

"I drove half an hour out of my way to see you," Dad told me bitterly.

"Sorry to be such a freakin' inconvenience," I snapped back. "Nobody asked you to."

The anger in my voice made it wobble, and Anders pushed my balled fist open and threaded his fingers between mine, then gave my hand a gentle squeeze. He was making it even harder to breathe, but I never wanted him to let go.

Dad's eyes dropped to our intertwined hands, and he shook his head, finally realising that he was beaten. "Fine. I'll come by later and take you to dinner. We really need to talk."

As if I'd go. Dad didn't give me a chance to argue though, turning on his heel after one last look at Anders, and striding back to his SUV.

Anders released my hand. "You okay?"

I nodded, but the adrenalin was flooding out of my body and I felt strangely teary all of a sudden.

"Yeah. Thanks for that. He's…" I couldn't find the words to describe how awful my father was, so I just shrugged.

Anders gave a sympathetic half-smile. "Parents, eh? C'mon. I promised I'd take you home, so I guess I'd better. But if it's okay with you, I've got a detour in mind."

His idea of a detour turned out to be the drive-thru at Burger King. Not exactly the most romantic venue, but somehow he'd made sitting in a car wiping mayonnaise off his chin look hot.

"Come on, eat up," he told me, and I forced another tepid French fry into my mouth. I hated fast food, and I knew it was going to make me feel sick later, but I couldn't say no to him.

"I'm not all that hungry," I told him, ignoring the greasy burger that was sitting at the bottom of the paper bag on my lap.

"And here I thought I was saving you from dinner with your old man." He shot me a suspicious look. "You're not on a diet, are you?"

I shook my head slowly, but had to ask. "What's wrong with a diet?"

"Waste of time. Life's for living, not starving yourself. Besides, you don't need to diet. If you get any skinnier, I won't be able to see you from side on."

I pushed three more fries into my mouth and forced myself to chew. "I'm not on a diet. I'm just not a big eater, that's all."

I thought about Molly then, and hoped she was okay.

Wondered if she was eating properly, and whether Susannah would notice if she wasn't.

Wondered if she missed me as much as I missed her.

9

TRUE STORY

I pushed Molly determinedly to the back of my mind for the rest of the week, trying in vain to distract myself with schoolwork, riding the ponies I had left, doctoring Lucas and Robin as best as I could and helping AJ train Squib. But I had too much restless energy and nowhere to direct it, and in eventual frustration, I got up early on Tuesday morning and went for a run. I've never been much of a sports enthusiast, but I found that running helped me to relax. The rhythm of my feet slapping against the tarmac was strangely hypnotic, and only when my lungs were bursting and I was struggling to draw in breath did I stagger back to a walk, hands on hips and dragging in oxygen, waiting for my heart rate to return to some semblance of normal. Then I was off again, running until I was red in the face and dripping with sweat. Then home and straight into the shower, letting the hot water ease my aches and pains.

I ran before school and in the evenings, after the ponies had been ridden and the boxes been mucked out, before collapsing at the kitchen table to do my homework. I soon discovered that if I hadn't been for a run, I couldn't think straight. If I hadn't run, my legs went all jittery and I kept feeling strange waves of panic washing over me, trying to drown me in some kind of inexplicable anxiety. Sitting still, I felt trapped. But when I was running, I felt free.

Dad wore Mum down eventually, and on Friday night he turned up at the door and again insisted on taking me out for dinner. Both of my parents ignored my protests about being blindsided, and when I went into my room and slammed the door, Mum came after me.

"Katy, would you just do this, please? For me?"

I stared at her, my planned protestations about how I shouldn't have to spend time with the man dying on my lips. "For *you*?"

"Yes. He won't stop ringing me and demanding to see you. So can you go with him tonight to get him out of my hair? Just be your usual self, and I'm sure he won't want anything to do with either of us by the time you're through."

Ouch. She was kidding, sort of, but it still stung. Even my mother thought I was hard to love. There's a ringing endorsement for you.

I was tired of arguing. "Fine, whatever. Get out of here while I get changed."

Mum walked off with a smug look on her face while I dragged a pair of jeans and a reasonably clean white top on, shoved my feet into the cowboy boots that I'd bought last summer but kept losing the confidence to wear, because I felt like they made me stand out too much. I decided not to care anymore, and I liked the boots. Besides, they were the only heels I owned, and

I wanted to be as tall and sophisticated as possible tonight. I found some lipstick and brushed my hair out, then marched down the hall into the kitchen where my father was waiting.

He took me to a steak house, a loud and family-friendly venue with waitresses in jeans and red polo shirts. The rugby was playing on a screen on the wall, and Dad kept shooting surreptitious glances at it when he thought I wasn't looking. I wanted to tell him that if he wanted to see the game he should've just stayed home and watched it, but didn't want to initiate any conversation, so I kept my mouth shut.

"Are you ready to order?"

The waitress was young and blonde and I wondered if she was my father's type. He ordered while I stared down at the menu in my hands and wondered what on earth I was going to eat. They were both looking at me now, the waitress' pen poised over her pad, Dad staring expectantly at me. Waiting for a decision.

I ran my eye down the list of menu options again. "What do you have that's vegetarian?"

The waitress looked taken aback at the thought of someone who didn't eat meat coming to a steak house, and Dad frowned at me.

"You're not a vegetarian."

"How would you know?" I challenged him, and he shot an apologetic look at the waitress.

"Your mother never said anything," he replied, looking a bit worried. *Well no, she wouldn't have, since I'd only just now decided to be vegetarian.* I didn't tell him that.

"We do a ranch salad," the waitress offered. "I can have them take the chicken and bacon out. I mean, prepare it without the chicken and bacon. If you'd like."

"Fine, I'll have that." I was tempted to change my mind and order steak and chips, just to mess with them, but I couldn't be bothered. I handed the menu back to the girl, who hurried off gratefully to the kitchen, and Dad rested his elbows on the table and steepled his fingers together, looking at me like I was some strange new specimen that had just been discovered.

"What did you want to talk about?" *Might as well get it over with.*

"I wanted to talk to you."

"Well, I don't particularly want to talk to you," I told him.

He sighed. "I'm sorry, okay? I'm sorry I left. I'm sorry I didn't stick around, and I'm sorry that I didn't stay in touch, but I thought it would be for the best, in the long run."

"For the best?" I stared at him. "Seriously? Come on. Pull the other one, Dad." I hated saying that word, but I couldn't bring myself to call him Lionel. Even after all this time, it felt too weird. Besides, he should be reminded that he was my father. Even if he didn't want to be. "You want to talk, then talk. Let's start with telling me why you left." The waitress had been heading towards our table with a pitcher of water, but as my voice carried towards her, I saw her hesitate, then pivot and go back to the bar. *Probably safest.* "Wait, don't bother. I already got that memo. So she dumped you, huh?"

Dad frowned at me. "Who did?"

"Don't play games with me. The woman you left Mum for."

Dad blinked three times in rapid succession, and I felt my

heart clench. That was something that I did. I hadn't realised I got it from him.

"I didn't leave your mother for another woman. Who told you that?"

The vice around my heart squeezed tighter. "Yes you did. A younger, blonder, prettier…" My voice died away at the look on my father's face. I didn't like him and I didn't really trust him but I could tell that he was genuinely shocked by my comments.

"Did your mother…" He broke off and clenched his lips together tightly, looking away from me for a moment while he regained his composure. "I'm sorry if that's what Deb told you, but that's not what happened at all." He shook his head in frustration. "Unbelievable."

I wondered if he knew that if he started slagging off Mum in front of me, I'd be out of there like a robber's dog. "So what? You just got sick of us?" A horrible thought occurred to me, but I forced myself to say it out loud. "Was it me?" *Am I really that awful of a person that neither of my parents can stand me?*

To his credit, he was adamant about that. "No. Definitely not. Leaving you was the hardest part."

"So why then? Why just walk away?"

Dad took a deep breath and let it out slowly. Over his head, one of the rugby players onscreen was sprinting down field with the opposing team in hot pursuit. Half of the people in the restaurant were sitting on the edges of their seats, craning their necks towards the action.

"It wasn't you. It was your mother."

A ripple of sighs emanated from people around us as the

player was tackled a few metres short of the line. I didn't care about the game, but it was hard to look at Dad, because I had a sneaking suspicion that I wasn't going to like what he was about to tell me.

"You were so young, you didn't see it. But your mother and I had been having trouble for some time." The team in yellow turned the ball over, and one of the players in a red jersey got it. He dropped it onto his foot and it sailed downfield. I thought of Anders, and wondered if he'd be playing at that level one day. If he'd be on TV, and I'd be able to watch it and say *I know him.*

Dad was still talking. I didn't want to listen, but I couldn't help it. "She was never any good at managing her money. She might be better now, I don't know, but back then…" He shook his head, and I made reluctant eye contact with him.

She's not, I thought. Mum was always spending money we didn't have, which was part of the reason we didn't have a Molly fund, but I didn't want to admit to any weakness of hers in front of Dad.

"She stopped working after you were born, and relied heavily on my income. Not that I minded, but we were already living beyond our means, so I was forced to fold my business and take a job in Napier. I didn't really want to, didn't like the job or the boss, but the money was good and I wanted to provide for my family. I did my best, Katy."

The waitress brought our food then, and Dad thanked her. I picked up my fork and prodded at the salad, which was covered in thick ranch dressing. My stomach clenched at the sight of it, and I set my fork down again.

"But your mother spent the money as fast as I made it, and we never seemed to be able to climb out of debt. When we found the farm, I was relieved at first. It was small enough to be affordable, even if we'd have to scrimp a bit on other costs, and it would be years before we could do any renovations to the house. Deb agreed readily when I told her that we'd have to stop spending money if we bought the place, but once we'd moved in, she was back to her old ways."

My throat was dry, and I wished the waitress had had the guts to bring us that pitcher of water. Dad cut a piece off his steak and raised it halfway to his mouth, then kept talking.

"I've always been careful with money. I've had to be. My family was never flush, but my parents lived well within their means, so that there was always enough for us to be comfortable. They hadn't approved of Deb in the first place, thought she was too flaky, and maybe they were right. But…"

"But she was pregnant," I filled in. The rugby team in red jerseys were running hard, and I watched the ball be flicked from one player to the next, quick as lightning, barely landing in someone's hands before being sent to the next. They ran in formation, weaving past the hapless opposition until finally one of the players side-stepped his way past the guy in yellow and dived across the line, driving the ball down into the grass. A chorus of moans and grumbles filled the restaurant, and Dad's eyes flickered to the screen behind me.

"You were saying?"

"She was pregnant," he nodded. "And you were such a beautiful baby. I was so proud of you." I wished he'd stop talking in the past tense. "I wanted you to have everything, but Deb was making it impossible for me to save for the things you really needed. Education. Travel. All of the opportunities I wanted to give you."

"You never wanted me to have ponies," I reminded him. I shoved a bit of lettuce into my mouth and chewed. The dressing stuck to my tongue, and I had to force myself to swallow.

"I think it's great that you had ponies," Dad contradicted me. "You loved them – still do, by the looks of it. And that's fantastic, and I'm so proud of how good you are. I've seen all your winnings, and I'm impressed. But I admit, I didn't see why an eight-year-old needed five ponies. They were taking up every spare second of your life. I barely saw you. And when I wasn't working, you and your mother were off at horse shows, travelling up and down the country."

Some excuse that was. "You could've come with us."

He shrugged. "I'm not much of a horseman, you know that. And I wanted us to have something else, something separate. Something that was ours, because I was already aware that my relationship with your mother wasn't going to last the distance, and I didn't want to lose you when it came apart. But Deb had you under her thumb, and no matter how hard I tried, I couldn't find a way in."

The rugby players jogged off the field for halftime, and I finally looked at my father's earnest expression.

"Did you fight for me? After you left. Did you try and see me?"

"You don't remember?"

I shook my head, and Dad blinked again, three times in swift succession. I wished he'd stop doing that, even though I

127

knew he couldn't help it.

"Of course I tried. But on the few occasions that I managed to wrestle you away from her, you retreated into a little shell and would hardly talk to me. We had nothing in common, and the one time I tried to get you to spend the night away from her, you cried until I took you home."

"I got homesick," I muttered, feeling a hot flush fill my cheeks.

I didn't want to admit to him that homesickness was something that still affected me at times. Stupid, at my age, but not something I'd yet managed to completely control.

"I didn't know if it was that, or because you hated me, or that she'd made you so dependant on her that you couldn't be away from her for more than a few hours at a time. And then I got the job offer in Wellington, so I moved down there. I didn't want to, but the money was good and I needed to pay my debts somehow before I ended up completely bankrupt."

"It can't have been that bad."

"It was close. Everything was in my name, but she had full access to my account. Stupid of me not to cut her off, but she refused to be one of those women who are only given an allowance by their husbands, and I couldn't bring myself to do that either. It seemed too unfair, and controlling. But when she bought that horse truck without even asking me, knowing that we couldn't afford it…" He shook his head. "That was the straw that broke the camel's back. That was when I knew I had to leave or we'd end up with nothing left at all."

He started eating his steak and I picked at my salad as his words sunk in. He was right about Mum being hopeless with money. We didn't have much, so we had to be reasonably careful, but I could imagine the temptation for her of a seemingly bottomless bank account that she had full access to. I started remembering more things. Hearing them fight, yelling and slamming doors, Dad angrily shouting that I didn't need any more ponies and Mum saying that she was only buying them to make me happy, and if he knew his daughter at all he wouldn't want to take her happiness away from her. I'd hide out in the stables until they were done, petrified that Dad would get his way and the ponies would be sold. That was why I'd always been on Mum's side, and why I'd always been nervous around my father. He was always angry, or so it had seemed to me. Mum would reassure me that he'd be fine, he was just grumpy but he loved us really and he wanted us to have the ponies. I think she'd genuinely had herself convinced, and I wondered if she'd seen his departure coming at all.

And I remembered the fighting after we'd bought the truck. Mum and I had found it for sale online, and we'd both been so excited about it that she'd decided she couldn't wait for Dad to get home and give his permission. She'd called the owner that afternoon, and bought the truck before Dad even realised the money had left his account.

"You tried to return it. The truck," I said, and Dad looked confused at first, then nodded.

"I did. We couldn't afford it."

I kept my eyes on his. "But we kept it."

He nodded. "Leaving was bad enough. I didn't want you to lose anything else, so I took out the necessary loan and paid it off."

"Why did you move to Australia?"

"Work. Big money over there, working on the gas pipeline. Hard work and long hours, but meals and accommodation were included. I worked hard and only spent what money I had to. Made it easy to save."

"You didn't think child support was necessary?" I asked bitterly.

Dad looked guilty as he finished his steak and set down his knife. "I wanted to be sure the money would go to you, for things you needed. Not to your mother to fritter away on those bloody horses." I narrowed my eyes at him, and he sensed that he'd taken a misstep, but carried on. "I set up a bank account for you, put what I could into it. You'll get the money once you're eighteen."

"And if I decide to spend it on more bloody horses?"

Dad sighed. "Then that'll be your decision. But I hope you'll have more sense when the time comes."

"Yeah, well. Chances aren't good." The rugby players ran back onto the field, ready for the game to resume. "Can we go now? I'm tired."

Dad looked at my plate. "You've barely eaten."

"I don't like it. It tastes weird. Sorry," I added, thinking of the money he'd wasted. Clearly that was something he cared deeply about. "I'll have something when I get home."

He hesitated, then pushed his chair back from the table and stood up. "Okay. We can go."

10

AMENDS

We didn't go to any shows that weekend. Wairarapa 2* was on, but it wasn't worth travelling all that way with only Forbes and Puppet in the truck. And Squib, I supposed, but I'd told Mum that I didn't feel like showing that weekend. She'd immediately felt my forehead and asked if I was okay, which had only made me snap at her that maybe I was getting sick of traipsing around the shows all the time, and would it kill her to let me have a weekend off?

I'd almost meant it at the time, but had soon discovered that I didn't know how to entertain myself over a weekend if I wasn't competing. After riding Forbes and Puppet, hand-walking Robin and going for a long run, I'd taken AJ up on her offer of a sleepover, which was how I'd ended up sitting on the couch in her family room, watching *Mean Girls* and thinking about Anders.

I'd barely seen him since the day he'd given me a ride home. Our paths didn't cross much at school, and AJ had started to get suspicious when I'd kept asking after him, so I'd had to stop. As much as I liked him, my unrequited crush wasn't worth putting my friendship with AJ in jeopardy. I'd hoped to see him when I arrived at her house, but he'd been miles away at rugby training in New Plymouth, and hadn't arrived home until half an hour ago. He'd stuck his head into the room and said hi, grabbed a handful of our popcorn despite AJ's protestations, then yawned and gone off to bed before I'd had a chance to say more than "Hi" back to him. So now I was watching a movie that I'd seen a thousand times before, fighting off my own yawns as the clock ticked closer and closer towards midnight.

Finally the movie ended, and AJ dumped the popcorn dregs into the rubbish bin, and I stood up and stretched and thought longingly of my bed at home. The airbed on the floor of AJ's room – a room she shared with Astrid – really wasn't conducive to a good night's sleep. I could feel the old homesickness creeping up on me, and I desperately tried to fight it. Homesickness was stupid. Only little kids got homesick, and I was fifteen now. Way too old for that crap.

AJ opened the back door and followed Dax out into the dark, ready to shut him into his kennel run for the night, and suddenly I missed Critter. Missed his little claws scrabbling across the floor, missed his soft little snores as he curled up against me at night, missed the way he licked my chin when I cuddled him.

Stop it. Pull yourself together. I smiled at AJ as she came back into the house and locked the door behind her, then followed her into her bedroom and grabbed my pyjamas, then went into the bathroom and changed. I brushed my teeth, washed my face, combed out my hair. Stared at my reflection in the mirror, wishing that I was prettier, that my face wasn't so narrow and pinched-looking, that my hair was thicker and wavier. At least my skin was good, I supposed, throwing everything back into my toiletries bag and creeping across the dark hallway and into AJ's room.

She had the lamp on next to her bed, ignoring her sister who was softly snoring on the other side of the room. AJ tossed her phone down onto her bed as I came in, and went out to brush her own teeth. I reached for the sleeping bag that was still rolled up on AJ's bed, and my eye caught the picture on her phone just before it disappeared.

Swallowing hard, I picked the phone up and swiped the screen back into life. Fortunately for me, AJ didn't keep her phone password protected, and it took me straight back to the Facebook app. The photo was exactly what I'd thought it was, and it hit me in the gut like a sucker punch. Susannah. Molly. A bright blue sash around the pony's neck. A smug smile on her rider's face. A caption that burned my heart to read. *Meet Molly, the latest addition to our team. Finished a v close 2nd in the 1.20 at Wairarapa today. Love her already!*

I couldn't tear my eyes away from the picture. As I scrolled down, I bumped the comments section with my thumb, and another screen popped up. *8 people like this.* I felt a moment of satisfaction at that. Susannah had posted the pic two hours ago, and only eight people liked it. If I'd posted that pic, I'd have had over a hundred likes within an hour. But then, Susannah didn't have many friends.

I ran my eye down the comments, and then got another kick in the gut as I saw AJ's name. *Well done and go Molly, she looks so happy with you,* she'd written. And Susannah had liked her comment, and posted a reply. I couldn't bring myself to click on that. I didn't want to know what she had to say. The only thing I wanted to know was what the hell was going on, and when had my best friend started Facebooking my worst enemy?

AJ came back into the room then, and I stared at her, my hand shaking. I'd *told* her, time and time and time again, what a terrible person Susannah was. And even if she wasn't, what was AJ doing congratulating her on her success on *my* pony?

She's not your pony anymore, the voice in my head reminded me. *SHUT UP!* I told it as I threw her phone back onto the bed and faced my friend.

"I want to go home."

AJ had the grace to look guilty, knowing exactly what I'd seen. "Did you…Katy, I'm sorry. But I wanted to see how she was. Keep tabs on her, and I knew you wouldn't, so – "

It didn't make it okay. None of this was okay. "I have to go home now."

AJ frowned at me. "Shh! Everyone's in bed."

She looked at her sister, whose snoring had ceased. I didn't care if Astrid woke up. I didn't care if the whole houseful of them woke up. I couldn't stay here any longer. I pulled my phone out of my bag and rang Mum, my fingers still shaking. AJ sat on her bed and muttered apologies at me, offering to delete her comment to Susannah, to unfriend or block her, but I ignored her. The damage was done.

Come on, pick up! The phone rang, and rang. Eventually it went to voicemail, and I hung up in frustration, then tried Mum's cell. AJ had quit trying to talk me out of leaving, and I tucked my knees up into my chest as I listened to the phone connect. It didn't even ring – just went straight to voicemail

134

as well. What the hell? Where was she? A rising tide of panic swept over me. I was trapped here. I had to stay. I couldn't stay.

I got up and left the room, ignoring AJ's whispered pleas to stay, and went straight to Anders's bedroom. I was beyond caring about anything right now other than finding someone who would drive me home, and I knocked firmly. AJ was watching me from her doorway, and I saw her shake her head slowly as I knocked again.

Anders opened the door. His hair was rumpled and he was only wearing a loose pair of boxer shorts. A fleeting sense of embarrassment washed over me, before I thought about what would happen if I couldn't convince him to give me a ride. I'd have to ring a taxi or risk waking AJ's parents, or…

"What's wrong?" Anders had that same concerned look on his face that he'd had a few days ago at the sports field, and he leaned past me and looked towards AJ's room, but she was gone.

"Can you take me home?" I couldn't stop the thickness in my voice, and I realised with disgust that I was going to cry soon.

Why did I have to be so pathetic? I couldn't even tell anymore if it was anger at AJ or bitterness towards Susannah or disappointment in Molly or just the overwhelming homesickness that was making me so emotional. All I knew was that I couldn't control it, no matter how hard I tried.

Anders was nodding. "Sure. Give me a sec to get dressed."

He pushed the door almost shut, just leaving a crack of light showing, and I stood in the dark hallway and waited. When he opened it again, he had jeans and a hoodie on, and his car keys dangled from his fingertips.

"Let's go." He flicked his light switch off, leaving us in the dark, then put a hand on my shoulder and guided me towards the front door. Then he stopped, and glanced back up the hall. "Wait here. I'm just going to check on Poss."

"She's fine." I shivered, suddenly aware that I was wearing pyjamas with dolphins on them, and my feet were bare.

But Anders had already walked away, his own bare feet travelling soundlessly across the carpeted floor, and I shifted my weight restlessly as I waited for him to return.

It didn't take long. He was back in moments with my overnight bag slung over his shoulder, and he unlocked the front door and held it open for me as I stepped out into the dark, cool night.

We didn't talk much on the way home. Anders rubbed his eyes a couple of times and yawned, but just shook his head when I apologised for dragging him out of bed.

"Don't worry about it. Happens."

I didn't know exactly what he meant by that. I supposed it depended on what AJ had told him had happened, but I couldn't bring myself to get into it. I just wanted to get home.

When we pulled up in front of my house at last, I let out a breath that I didn't know I'd been holding. Everything was back where it should be. I opened the car door and smelled the familiar scent of horses and hay and grass, and heard Lucas shifting around in his stable, bored by his long confinement.

"Thanks."

"All good." Anders reached into the back seat and pulled my bag out, passing it to me as I stepped out of the car, the stones biting into my bare feet. I'd left my shoes at their house, but I didn't care. "Sure you're okay?"

I nodded, glancing across towards the house. It was only then that I noticed that not everything was where it was meant to be. Mum's car was missing. Anders must've seen the frown on my face, because he asked me again what was wrong.

"Mum's not here. I didn't realise she was going out." I leaned back into the car and looked at the dashboard clock. Almost midnight. She was never out this late, and a bad feeling settled over me. "That's weird."

Anders gazed past me, looking at the empty house. "Want me to stay with you 'til she gets back?"

I was tempted to say yes, but I shook my head. "It's okay. You should get home, get some sleep. I've got a key."

"Sure?"

I nodded, even though I wasn't. Then I caught a glimpse of headlights coming up our driveway, and we both turned to see Mum's car coming bouncing over the potholes. She dimmed her lights as we squinted at her, and parked next to the house. I pulled my bag out and hefted it onto my shoulder.

"She's home now. Thanks again. I owe you one."

I caught a flash of Anders's grin right before Mum flicked her headlights off and we were plunged back into darkness. "I'll hold you to that."

I shut the car door and he reversed out as I walked over to the house. Mum was out of her car and watching me approach, looking puzzled.

"Are you okay?"

"I'm fine. Would people stop asking me that?" I didn't mean

to snap at her, but it just came out. "I just felt like coming home, that's all."

Mum was giving me a suspicious look, like she knew I was homesick again and wanted to remind me that I should be over that by now, so I pushed past her and went to the front door, shivering in the cold. She noticed that, at least, so unlocked the door and flicked the light on. Critter came scrabbling over to meet us, and I scooped him up and hugged him tight as I went straight to my room and fell into bed, exhausted.

Critter woke me up by licking my face, and I pushed him off.

"Gross," I muttered, rolling over onto my other side and trying to ignore him. But he jumped off the bed and scrabbled at the door, and I knew if I didn't get up soon there would be a wet patch on the carpet. Groaning, I got up and let him out, then decided that I might as well go for a run.

When I got home, Dad was there. I still wasn't sure how I felt about everything he'd told me, but I knew that I wasn't up for another heart-to-heart. I was still a little out of breath as he got out of his car and smiled tentatively at me.

Mum's not home, I realised, and I wondered where she could be. The truck was gone too, and then I remembered her saying something about getting the mechanic to look at it this morning.

"Been for a run?"

Duh. I just nodded, and he shifted his weight onto the other foot.

"I have to head up to Auckland," he told me. "Got a job interview up there."

So much for moving back here then. And just when I'd started to think I might be able to handle having him around.

"Okay," I said noncommittally.

"I wanted to give you this," he said, reaching into the car, and my heart pounded in anticipation for a moment before he pulled out a white envelope and handed it to me. "For your birthday."

Oh yeah. My birthday was in three days' time. I took the envelope from him, wishing it was my eighteenth and not my sixteenth, and that the envelope meant access to the child support he owed me. Well, he was going to have to start paying that soon anyway, now that he was back in the country. Unless the Auckland interview was for another overseas job…

"Thanks." I held the envelope tightly, feeling the crease of thin cardboard inside it. It wasn't thick enough to have a wad of cash inside it, not that it mattered now. The one thing I'd wanted money for was already gone. "I need to take a shower."

"Okay." Dad hovered for a moment as though he wanted to hug me, so I took a step backwards.

"See ya."

Inside the house, I threw the card down onto the coffee table without opening it, and took a long hot shower. My fingers were starting to wrinkle by the time I finally stepped out. I heard the rumble of our truck engine coming up the driveway.

That'll be Mum home. I dried off and pulled on some clothes, then wandered back into the lounge and flopped down onto the couch as she came inside.

"Morning."

"Hey." I looked around for the TV remote, but I couldn't

see it. Mum shifted her weight restlessly, a strange expression on her face.

"Is your father here?"

"Do you see his car?" I asked. "Been and gone. How'd you know?"

Mum shrugged. "He said he was going to come by and wish you a happy birthday."

"He did that. Now he's off to a job interview." I picked up the bent envelope and waved it at her. "Left me this, though. Aren't I lucky?"

"What is it?"

"A card, I'm guessing."

Sick of the inquisition, I got up and went into the kitchen. Mum followed me, watching as I pulled a banana out of the fruit bowl and peeled it, then took a bite.

"Aren't you going to open it?"

I looked sceptically at the card that I'd tossed onto the bench. "What's the point? It's just a card."

"You don't know that for sure," Mum replied, so just to shut her up, I tore the envelope open and pulled the card out. It had a horse on the front. *Nice try, Dad.* The horse looked a bit like Molly. I opened it, half-hoping that a cheque would fall out, but nothing. Only a brief scrawl in Dad's handwriting underneath the printed happy birthday message.

For all the ones I've missed. Love, Dad.

"Seriously?" I asked Mum. "One card, for everything he missed?"

Mum shrugged. "Oh well. I picked up some feed while I had the truck out, would you go and unload it for me? My

140

shoulder's playing up again."

"Fine." Lugging heavy feed sacks around actually sounded appealing right now. Something tough and physical to take my mind off how much of a disappointment my father had proven to be, yet again.

The truck was parked in the middle of the yard, and I looked critically at it as I walked up to the ramp. *Your fault,* I told the hapless vehicle. *You're the straw that broke the camel's back.* Although if it hadn't been the truck, it would've been something else. That much was obvious, at least now. I undid the clip at the back and hit the button that would lower the hydraulic ramp, my thoughts still wandering. *At least he let us keep it. That can't have been easy.* The ramp settled onto the gravel with a crunch, and I took a step up onto it, then stopped and stared.

There weren't any feed bags in the truck. But there was a bay pony with a white star, staring back at me with her ears pricked.

"Molly?" She nickered a welcome to me, and I was up the ramp and inside the truck before I realised my feet were moving. "Molly! What are you doing back?"

I pulled the lever back and pushed the partition out of the way, then unclipped her and led her to the top of the ramp, casting an eye over her as she walked. Was she injured? Had Susannah changed her mind? And why hadn't Mum told me that she'd just been to pick her up?

Mum was standing near the bottom of the ramp, shading her eyes with one hand as she looked up at me. My whole body was trembling as I stared back down at her, my thoughts in a confused whirlwind. Molly saw Lucas and let out an ear-splitting whinny, and Mum and I laughed.

"What's going on?" I asked my mother. "Is Molly back? Does she get to stay?"

Mum nodded. "She's all yours, sweetheart."

"Mine? But…how?" And then I noticed the crumpled card in my mother's hand, and I understood what it had really meant.

For all the ones I've missed.

I started crying then, the tears blurring my vision as I led my pony – *my* pony – down the ramp and into the paddock. I shut the gate behind her and leaned on it, not trusting my legs to hold me up as I watched Molly trot across the grass towards Forbes, who greeted her happily. She sniffed his nose for a moment, then laid her ears back and flung out a foreleg, squealing. I laughed through my tears and Mum came and stood next to me, putting an arm around my shoulders and holding me close.

"I think you'd better give your Dad a ring, don't you?"

I swallowed hard, and wiped my face. "Yeah. Do you have his number?"

Mum handed me the card again, with Dad's phone number scrawled on the back. I fished my cell phone out of my pocket and punched in the numbers, then watched as Mum walked back to the truck, leaving me to have the conversation in private. I stood there in the morning sun, still leaning on the gate, and smiled to myself as the phone began to ring.

♥

For more information, visit nzponywriter.com

Email nzponywriter@gmail.com and sign up to my mailing list for exclusive previews, new releases, giveaways and more!

Don't miss the next books in the Pony Jumpers series!

Pony Jumpers #3
TRIPLE BAR

Susannah Andrews has always been a keen competitor in the sport of show jumping. Spurred on by her parents, she was climbing the Grand Prix leader board with a firm eye on the top prize - until it all fell apart eighteen months ago. Refusing to give up on the sport she loves, and despite continued bullying on the circuit, she has pulled herself back into contention and is determined to prove herself once more.

But when her estranged brother contacts her after a lengthy absence, Susannah faces a tough choice. Can she forgive him for what he did - and if she does, will her parents ever speak to her again?

♥

Pony Jumpers #4
FOUR FAULTS

Tess Maxwell never really wanted to be a competition rider, and she certainly never wanted to inherit her sister Hayley's difficult Grand Prix pony Misty Magic. But nobody ever listens to what Tess wants, and despite her resolution never to ride Misty again, she finds herself back in the saddle as he continues to tear her confidence to shreds.

After her parents decide that Misty will be sold after Christmas unless Tess changes her mind, she has more to contend with than just surviving the next seven weeks. Because Hayley is determined not to let her beloved pony leave the farm, and she doesn't care what it will take to change her sister's mind…

Pony Jumpers #5
FIVE STRIDE LINE

AJ is still dreaming of taking her talented pony Squib to the top level of pony show jumping, but she's about to hit some serious roadblocks. Squib has started slipping on the turns, and now her best friend Katy is insisting that AJ needs to put shoes on Squib, instead of letting him jump barefoot as he's always done before. But AJ isn't so sure…

Can AJ achieve her goals without compromising what she feels is best for her pony?

♥

Pony Jumpers #6
SIX TO RIDE

Katy's father has returned, and he wants to be more involved in her life. Although she's reluctant at first to welcome him back, her head is turned when he offers to buy her a new horse for Christmas. And not just any horse – a talented youngster with all the scope and talent to take her to the top.

But Katy is finding her dream horse a challenge to ride, and as the pressure to succeed mounts from all sides, she can feel herself starting to crack…

ACKNOWLEDGEMENTS

Many thanks to Paula Riepen for the use of the cover image.

If you liked this story, please also check out the rest of the series, and my four full-length novels, also available on Amazon. There are some familiar faces in those books, as everything I write ties into each other, so although they are focused on different characters, quite a few of the people you have met in *First Fence* and *Double Clear* appear in previous (and upcoming) books.

For more about me and the books I have written, you can visit my website at **nzponywriter.com**, where you can sign up for my mailing list to get new release information, updates and enter giveaways. You can also find me on Facebook as **Kate Lattey - Author** and on Instagram at **@kate_lattey**.

Finally, if you enjoyed reading this book, please consider leaving a review on Amazon or Goodreads to encourage others to give it a try.

ABOUT THE AUTHOR

Kate Lattey lives in Waikanae, New Zealand and started riding at the age of 10. She was lucky enough to have ponies of her own during her teenage years, and competed regularly in show jumping, eventing and mounted games before finishing college and heading to university, graduating with a Bachelor of Arts in English & Media Studies.

In the years since, she has never been far from horses, and has worked in various jobs including as a livery yard groom in England, a trekking guide in Ireland, a riding school manager in New Zealand, and a summer camp counselor in the USA. It was during her time there that Kate started writing short stories about the camp's horses, which were a huge hit with the campers, and inspired Kate to continue pursuing her passion for writing.

Kate currently owns a Welsh Cob x Thoroughbred gelding named JJ, and competes in show jumping and show hunter competitions, as well as coaching at Pony Club and judging at local events.

She has been reading and writing pony stories ever since she can remember, and has many more yet to come! If you enjoyed this book, check out the rest of the series and her other novels on Amazon, and visit nzponywriter.com to sign up for her mailing list and get information about new and upcoming releases.

DARE TO DREAM

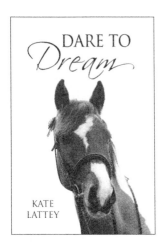

Saying goodbye to the horses they love has become a way of life for Marley and her sisters, who train and sell show jumpers to make their living. Marley has grand ambitions to jump in Pony of the Year, but every good pony she's ever had has been sold out from under her to pay the bills.

Then a half-wild pinto pony comes into her life, and Marley finds that this most unlikely of champions could be the superstar she has always dreamed of. As Marley and Cruise rise quickly to the top of their sport, it seems as though her dream might come true after all.

But her family is struggling to make ends meet, and as the countdown to Pony of the Year begins, Marley is forced to face the possibility of losing the pony she has come to love more than anything else in the world.

Can Marley save the farm she loves, without sacrificing the pony she can't live without?

DREAM ON

"Nobody has ever tried to understand this pony.
Nobody has ever been on her side. Until now.
She needs you to fight for her, Marley. She needs you to love her."

Borderline Majestic was imported from the other side of the world to bring her new owners fame and glory, but she is almost impossible to handle and ride. When the pony lands her rider in intensive care, it is up to Marley to prove that the talented mare is not dangerous - just deeply misunderstood.

Can Marley dare to fall in love again to save Majestic's life?

This much-anticipated sequel to *Dare to Dream* was a Top 20 Kindle Book Awards Semi-Finalist in 2015.

Clearwater Bay #1
FLYING CHANGES

When Jay moves from her home in England to live with her estranged father in rural New Zealand, it is only his promise of a pony of her own that convinces her to leave her old life behind and start over in a new country.

Change doesn't come easily at first, and Jay makes as many enemies as she does friends before she finds the perfect pony, who seems destined to make her dreams of show jumping success come true.

But she soon discovers that training her own pony is not as easy as she thought it would be, and her dream pony is becoming increasingly unmanageable and difficult to ride.

Can Jay pull it all together, or has she made the biggest mistake of her life?

Clearwater Bay #2
AGAINST THE CLOCK

It's a new season and a new start for Jay and her wilful pony Finn, but their best laid plans are quickly plagued by injuries, arguments and rails that just won't stay in their cups. And when her father introduces her to his new girlfriend, Jay can't help wondering if her life will ever run according to plan.

While her friends battle with their own families and Jay struggles to define hers, it is only her determination to bring out the best in her pony that keeps her going. But after overhearing a top rider say that Finn's potential is being hampered by her incompetent rider, Jay is besieged by doubts in her own ability…and begins to wonder whether Finn would be better off without her.

Can Jay bear to give up on her dreams, even if it's for her pony's sake?

Printed by Amazon Italia Logistica S.r.l.
Torrazza Piemonte (TO), Italy

12778904R00089